MISTLETOE BABY

A CRESCENT COVE BITE

TARYN QUINN

This book is a work of fiction. The names, characters, places, and incidents are products of the writer's imagination or have been used fictitiously and are not to be construed as real. Any resemblance to persons, living or dead, actual events, locales or organizations is entirely coincidental.

Mistletoe Baby
© 2021 Taryn Quinn
Rainbow Rage Publishing

Cover by LateNite Designs
Photograph by Shutterstock

First print edition: February 2021
ISBN Print edition: 978-1-940346-68-7

PLAYLIST

Billie Eilish: everything i wanted
David Cook: I'm About to Come Alive
Michael Bublé: Christmas(Baby Please Come Home)
Bishop Briggs: Hi-Lo (Hollow)
Hozier: As It Was
Alexander Jean: Dreams

FULL PLAYLIST ON SPOTIFY
Please check out our website for more details!

To mistletoe magic.

ONE

BLASTING MICHAEL BUBLÉ'S VERSION OF "SILENT NIGHT" AS I SPED DOWN the street in an icy winter wonderland probably seemed incongruous, but I was in an exceptionally good mood.

Who wouldn't be when classes at the community college were officially finished for the semester? Finals were done. Grades submitted. Endless infernal staff meetings in the bag.

I was finally free—for a month or so, give or take some faculty enrichment days.

I'd cracked the windows on my wholly-inappropriate-for-this-climate Toyota Supra sports car to let in the cool late afternoon breeze, and I'd put the heat on low to offset the chill. I was driving a little too fast for the fat flakes streaming down from the sky and accumulating in frosty slush along the side of the roadway. Playing my music a bit too loud for the quaint small town I was headed toward full bore.

Crescent Cove, was it? I'd never been here before. Oh, I'd heard of it, considering I lived fifty-plus miles away. But this place was postcard bucolic, a speck on the map, and I tended to like to hit the highways where I could go faster.

Thirty miles an hour was not fast. Nor was my risky thirty-six.

I didn't even know why I'd driven this far out today. I was all too

1

used to Central New York's changeable weather. Snowstorms didn't usually slow me down, but the sleet gray clouds warned we might be in for a prolonged event.

So much for enjoying my freedom in my sweet impractical beauty. I'd just do a U-turn and head back—

Suddenly, a truck backed out of a driveway, and I hit the brakes far too hard. My tires shrieked as I aimed right for the curb—and the ditch hidden by the thick layer of white layered on top of it.

My horn rang out as did my particularly colorful stream of curses. Wheels spun. My knee jabbed hard into something, and for a second, my vision wavered.

Had I hit my head? Or had the belt tightened just enough to send my ribcage upward into my skull?

Could've been either one.

Michael kept singing as I shut my eyes against the pain in my leg. I could probably walk it off. All in all, I'd gotten off easy. My poor baby though. I didn't want to see the damage.

Actually, I didn't want to deal with any of the crap that was now in my immediate future.

Next time? I'd circle my own block when I wanted to get my jollies in my almost-new car during the winter.

A sharp rap on my window had me opening my eyes and biting off a sigh. A guy wearing one of those hats with buffalo plaid flaps over his ears pressed his face up against the glass as I turned down the volume on the music and then lowered the window halfway. "You okay, fella? I didn't see you there as I was coming out."

I cocked a brow. Considering the non-neutral color of my car, I completely believed that. "I'm okay, thanks. You?"

I didn't know why I asked that. He hadn't driven off the road, I had. Because of him. And also because I'd recklessly been doing thirty-six.

This was why I so rarely colored outside the lines. It never ended well.

"Fine, fine. You got yourself some trouble here." He edged back to look at my crumpled fender, nose down in the ditch. "Want me to call Dare at Kramer and Burns Custom? He'll get you fixed right up in a jif."

This far out, my towing company would charge me a mint to come to my assistance. "Sure. I can call him." I tugged out my cell. "Kramer and Burns Custom, you said?"

"Have to turn down that loud music if you're going to call."

I ignored him as I searched Google and called. If he considered "Holly Jolly Christmas" set on low to be too loud, I couldn't help him.

And surprise, my good mood had fled at the same moment I'd crashed my freaking car.

"Good evening, Kramer speaking."

"Is this Dare?"

"No, this is his brother, Gage. Whatcha need?"

"Are all of you named like romance heroes?" Shockingly, he didn't respond. I cleared my throat. "I need a tow. I was referred by—"

I glanced at the window. The man and his ridiculous hat had disappeared. However, a cop was doing a U-turn to pull up beside me.

Fabulous.

"Anyway, can you come tow me?"

"Where are you?" His voice was appreciably cooler than when he'd answered the phone.

No one would accuse me of being wise, that was for sure. Made total sense to piss off the cavalry when I was well and truly stuck.

And I didn't know where I was.

I squinted through the snowy windshield. There was a street sign at the end of the block, but it was snowing too hard for me to make it out. Luckily, I could ask Officer Friendly.

He knocked on the window with his bare knuckles. "Had some trouble, I see."

"So everyone sees." When he frowned beneath the brim of his standard issue hat, I forced my shoulders to relax. "I'm on the phone with the tow place right now."

"Tell Dare Sheriff Brooks is on scene."

"Dare, Sheriff Brooks is on scene," I repeated into the phone, knowing I'd aggravate the guy on the end even more. I'd probably annoyed the sheriff too.

"Gage," the guy on the phone said testily. "Since you sound like an out-of-towner, ask Brooks where you are, and I'll send the truck out."

What had happened to that old adage that people in small towns were so easygoing? Probably required me not being a dick to them, but in my defense, my unscratched two-month-old car was now a mess.

My younger brother, Lennox, had warned me not to buy something that would depreciate so quickly.

Cars aren't an investment, Cal. Especially ones with a tawdry finish like yours.

Yeah, well, I'd clearly not listened. I'd loved my "tawdry" paint job that now would need to be retouched. And hey, bright side, with this accident, I'd done all the depreciating at once.

At least it had been minor. Shouldn't take long to fix.

""You still there, tourist?"

I frowned. Charming guy. "Why don't you just talk to the sheriff, rather than me playing telephone?" I attempted to hand the phone to the cop, but he shook his head and made a *gimme* gesture with his fingers.

I unclicked my belt and wrenched open the door, thankful that it seemed to be working correctly. The car was tilted at an angle, but with some finagling and shifting, I placed my boot on the cracked upper edge of the ditch and stepped out with assistance from the sheriff. I shut my door as the sheriff gave me my next orders.

"Tell Dare you're near the corner of East Lake Road and Grange."

I repeated the information into the phone and managed a "thank you" before Gage hung up on me.

Wasn't hospitality supposed to be a thing in small towns? I was beginning to think I'd been lied to.

First, Santa Claus was real. Then, small towns are wonderful, cozy places filled with lovely people.

The sheriff stepped back and eyed me up and down as he dipped his thumbs into the pockets of his trousers. "You're not from here."

Before I could reply to that incriminating statement—why it was incriminating, I wasn't sure, but there was no mistaking his tone—a float on the back of a flatbed truck rolled by, complete with a inflated bouncy house-style Santa's Workshop festooned with twinkling

Christmas lights and little animated elves climbing up and down ladders. The truck's driver blew the horn at the sheriff, and he waved, calling out a "Hey, Red, looking good," as the vehicle continued down the street at a speed approaching my own pre-crash.

Falling snow wasn't much of a deterrent around here. He'd better hope he didn't encounter Buffalo Plaid Hat Guy.

I looked around. Said guy and his truck were long gone.

"So?"

I pocketed my phone. "So what?"

"You're not from here," he repeated. "What's your business in Crescent Cove?"

"What, am I not allowed to drive through without a laminated pass? You should've asked the guy who pulled out in front of me why he couldn't watch where he was going."

The sheriff glanced at my awkwardly angled car, already gathering a healthy coating of snow. "Looks like you can't either."

I balled up my fists in the pockets of my long tweed coat. I shouldn't flip off the sheriff in a town I wasn't familiar with.

Problem was, I really, really wanted to.

"I was just out for a drive," I said defensively.

"Did you have a drink before you got behind the wheel?"

"No, but I wish I had." Okay, that definitely wasn't the right thing to say. It wasn't even what I'd meant. Exactly. "I mean, I should've had a drink and stayed home, rather than venturing out in this weather."

The sheriff crossed his arms over his quilted vest, pinned with some badge-looking thing he probably could've gotten at any dollar store. "Let's see some ID."

"Oh, for fuck's sake. How about ticketing the guy who caused me to slide?"

"Do you see him?" He made a show of looking around. "I don't."

"He stopped to talk to me, and then he left. How is that my fault?"

"Plate number?"

"I didn't see his plate."

"Description of the vehicle?"

"A big brown truck."

"UPS?"

"No, a SUV."

"Make and model?"

"I didn't have time to see all that. Big and boxy."

"Oh, well, now I can find him, no problem." He stared at me. "ID? Take it out, nice and slow."

"It's like I'm in an episode of *Law and Order,* if it was set in not-quite Mayberry." Shaking my head, I withdrew my wallet, took out my college ID, and handed it over.

He tipped back his hat. "Professor?"

"Yes."

"What do you teach?"

"Mythology and Applied Lessons in—"

"Good enough." Clearly disinterested, he returned my ID and nodded at my car. "Explains the bright yellow."

I tucked my ID away. "It does, does it?"

"License?"

"Are you kidding me? If I was out joyriding, I wouldn't have come here."

"I'll have you know Crescent Cove is known the state over. At this rate, we'll be known throughout the world."

I pulled out my license and gave it to him. "For what? Obnoxious floats?"

His jaw clicked as he studied my license. "Small-town charm and…"

"And what?"

"Procreation," he said in such a low voice I almost didn't hear him.

I didn't have time to ponder that inexplicable statement because a tow truck pulled up beside my car. A tall, bearded man in a baseball cap hopped down and flashed me a friendly smile that indicated he was *not* Gage Kramer and possible not even from this "quaint" Cove at all. "Hey there, I'm Dare Kramer. You are?"

"Callum MacGregor," I said as we shook hands. "Thanks for coming out so fast."

"In this weather, I figured you didn't want to be standing around. Hi, Brooks. How's that baby of yours?"

Brooks narrowed his eyes and said nothing. He was a charmer, this one.

Dare didn't seem deterred. "Caught the short straw today, huh?" He clapped the sheriff on the back. "Last I saw, Christian was on patrol."

"He's out too. All kinds of yahoos around tonight with the festival, and some of them can't stay on the road." With a narrowed-eyed stare for me, the sheriff returned my license. "I should give you a Breathalyzer."

I shrugged and put it away. "Do what you wish. It'd be a waste of your time, as I haven't had a drink since, at best guess, June sixteenth."

The night Hudson, my youngest brother—by seven and five minutes respectively from the other two triplets—had celebrated getting his degree in graphic design. He was considered the free-spirited one among my brothers, other than my own edgy sideline in drawing and painting.

Drawing and painting itself wasn't edgy, ignoring the whole starving artist thing. And I definitely was not starving after some of my recent commissions. But my choice of subject occasionally skirted the line for some.

Or *unskirted*, depending on my subject's state of undress.

Unusual faces and locations captured the bulk of my attention, so those were what I painted most often. It just seemed more notable the few times I'd painted a woman's form in a more natural way.

Well, notable to my family. The public at large didn't know who I was. I did my work, cashed my checks, and enjoyed my anonymity.

"We'll skip the Breathalyzer for now," the sheriff said, although he didn't seem happy about it.

Dare rubbed his gloved fingers over his bearded jaw. "She's a beaut. Shame she got scuffed up, but we'll get her in and out quick for you, with the holidays and all."

"Oh, thanks. I really appreciate that."

"Our shop does custom work. We'll fix her up so she looks better than brand new. Later on, how do you feel about racing stripes? My brother and Tish and their team do some damn fine work."

"Hmm. That might be an idea." Since I hadn't gotten off on the best foot with his brother, I'd probably end up with a middle finger painted on the fender, but why not give it a shot? "I'd like custom rims too."

"They'd look sweet with a ride like this. Tell you what, I'll bring it in and see what Gage and Tish think before we write you up a quote. We'll set you up with an appointment for the custom work in the new year. Or we can—" Dare broke off as yet another ginormous float went by, this one consisting of a huge gazebo decorated with Christmas lights. A sign proclaimed it courtesy of August and Kinleigh's Attic.

A flurry of honks went off as the driver moved into the opposite lane to pass our collection of vehicles on the side of the road, much to the sheriff's consternation.

"We need to get this car out of here. Talk at the shop. You keep it moving once your vehicle is ready." The sheriff pointed at me. "I don't want to hear about you causing another ruckus in town."

"I wasn't aware I'd caused a ruckus to begin with, but I'll take it under advisement." By this point, I couldn't do much other than shake my head.

At least I'd get an even more tricked out vehicle come the new year, even if it was at considerable cost. I could afford it. My account was nicely padded, and my agent thought a few more pieces would sell soon.

If I ever made it out of small town, USA. Hopefully, without a ticket. I wasn't even sure for what.

Sheriff Brooks would think of something.

"Okay, let's do this." Dare smiled. "You'll be on your way sooner than you think."

Ninety minutes later, I finally walked out of the auto shop. The snow was still thick and steady, but the townsfolk didn't seem to mind. The shop was just a bit down the street from what seemed to be a town square of sorts near the lake. The wide snow-covered lawn was covered with different food and game booths as well as the holiday floats I'd seen, plus a few others. People roamed around with their mittened hands clutching cups of cocoa, talking and laughing, accompanied by excited kids and scampering dogs.

Somehow I'd driven right into a Hallmark Christmas movie.

There was even the gazebo that had clearly served as the inspiration for the float that had glided past my damaged car. The real thing was even more grand as it gleamed in the darkness, strung with miles of lights and with a tree sparkling inside. Families clustered into the space to surround the tree, their laughter carrying on the crisp breeze. Someone pitched a snowball at a woman in the crowd, and she shrieked and rushed down the steps to build a snow arsenal of her own.

I smiled despite my general irritation. I'd been told I'd be able to pick my car up probably tomorrow, thanks to the hefty rush fee I'd paid. We'd scheduled the custom work for the new year.

At least I'd already secured lodging. After a recommendation from the shop, I'd called to reserve a room at The Hummingbird's Nest bed and breakfast down the block. The sprawling inn overlooked the frosty gleam of the lake and the Christmas hijinks going on nearby.

There was certainly plenty to inspire me here—even if cozy holiday scenes and frigid winter landscapes weren't my typical subject matter—but I didn't have any of my supplies. I definitely didn't have my laptop. Handily, I could take photos and sketch in my on-the-go app if I wanted to capture anything until I got back to my studio at home.

In the meantime, I'd just grab a slice of pizza from Dare's and Gage's dad's booth, Robbie's Pizza, at the winter festival. I'd heard it was the best in town. Of course Dare was entirely biased, but my growling stomach was willing to take his word for it.

Gage had neither confirmed or denied. He'd just written up my work order silently while giving me a healthy dose of side-eye worthy of my students.

Further cementing my daredevil status in town, I crossed the street outside the crosswalk and headed into the middle of carnival madness.

I bought two slices of cheese pizza and a bag of fried dough that steamed my glasses. Then I looked around the crowded square for a place to sit—or lean, since there was a half wall just beyond the gazebo attached to the pier. I found a spot and ate while I stared at the sprawling homes that lined the lake, their lit windows so homey and comforting in the snowy dark.

Something twisted in my chest that felt suspiciously like yearning. I didn't mind spending time alone. In fact, due to my large family, I'd grown to appreciate solitude. But being in the center of a happy crowd at Christmas reminded me that hey, there was more to life than teaching and grading and sketching and painting. More than Sunday dinners at my parents' house filled with friendly or not so friendly squabbling, depending on who was in a mood that week.

The holidays were coming up, and since I'd turned down my best friend Bryce's pathetic attempts to set me up on a blind date with one of her friends, I'd likely be alone.

Again.

"Hey, mister, you dropped your fried dough." A young girl with a dark ponytail and braces held out the bag of warm fried dough I hadn't realized I'd dropped.

I took it from her and smiled. "Thanks. Hey, do you want a piece? I can't eat it all."

But she was already walking away, back to her family.

Swallowing a sigh, I turned toward the gazebo and stared at the gigantic tree, its boughs weighed down with tinsel and ornaments. On the other side of the gazebo someone had hung a large sprig of mistletoe, and a woman stood beneath it, gazing up at the thing as if she couldn't understand what it was.

Or as if she was waiting for someone to kiss her.

Tufts of her light-colored hair—maybe pink?—stuck out in every direction from beneath her knit hat, as if her long braids had started unraveling in the wind. Her cheeks were ruddy from the cold and her unbuttoned coat flapped in the breeze, revealing a long, soft-looking dress. I couldn't decipher many other details about her, other than the lipstick-red scarf tossed jauntily over her shoulder.

She was cute. Maybe even beautiful if I could've made out more of her features in the darkness.

I threw out my empty plate and strode toward the gazebo steps, clutching my bag of fried dough as if it was a bouquet of roses.

I stopped on the top step. This was stupid. What was I even doing in this town? As soon as my car was ready, I'd drive away and never look back—except for coming back for my custom car work appointment. When I was in the mood for company, I was all about enjoying

Syracuse's city scene, visiting nightclubs and trendy eateries downtown. Most of the time, I simply didn't bother.

I definitely didn't approach random women in gazebos on a snowy night too close to Christmas, when my loneliness tasted like chalk in my throat.

Then she looked over at me and smiled, and I couldn't have stopped the forward motion of my feet if I'd tried.

I forgot the fried dough. Forgot the moms and dads and eager kids swarming about, pushing and nudging to get where they were going. That nameless woman drew me like the North star, a jewel glimmering in the darkness.

Words stuck in my head. I was usually so glib, so prepared with a ready remark. Not here. The dough slipped out of my hand as I reached her and simply lifted my hands to her icy-cold cheeks.

She was already rising on her tiptoes to meet me, her glossy pink lips parted and waiting.

We collided on a rush of breath, her mouth molding to mine as I gripped her jaw. I tilted her upward, taking her unspoken invitation and slipping my tongue inside. She sucked on the tip lightly, igniting a fire in under my skin as she rubbed against me. She fisted a handful of my coat, tugging at the material, bringing me down to her level so she could kiss me back with the same intensity.

She tasted like vanilla ice cream. Pure, sweet. Innocent somehow, as if she was daring me to break my control.

She didn't know she already had.

My teeth skimmed over her full lower lip, and she moaned as my hand moved of its own volition to her breast. I had the briefest sensation of its weight in my palm, round and perfect, before she tore her lips away.

Fuck, I'd gone too far.

She stared at me for a moment before darting around me and fleeing down the steps, her scarf slipping off and sliding to the ground.

"Wait." I followed and picked it up, but she never looked back.

I pressed my lips together. They were still tingling from the pressure of hers.

"It's mistletoe, you pervert." Someone jostled me from behind, and I turned to see I'd been bumped by an older woman's cane as she descended the steps. "Not a peep show."

She gave me another wack on the ankle for good measure before letting out a "harrumph" and shuffling down the walk.

I fingered the baby-soft scarf my mystery woman had left behind. She didn't know it, but I'd be sketching her tonight wearing this.

And only this.

TWO

My day was not off to a rip-roaring start. And it wasn't even the same day of the car-ditch mishap.

Maybe I'd finally learn that sweet small towns weren't necessarily meant for everyone.

"You don't recognize it?" I held up the bright red scarf as if it was the spoils from a prizefight. "Are you sure? It has your shop's tag right here." I jabbed at the embroidered *Kinleigh and August's attic* emblem near the fringe.

"No, I'm sorry." The woman who owned the store I was currently standing in glanced over her shoulder as a baby let out a wail. "That's my daughter. She needs lunch."

"Oh, okay, I'll wait while you give her a bottle or whatever."

Kinleigh smoothly pulled her long curly red hair over one shoulder. "Her lunch comes from my nipple."

I blinked. A sleepless night had left me on edge, and admittedly, I wasn't processing as fast as I would have normally. But that didn't compute for a good half a minute. "Oh. *Oh.*"

"Yes, *oh*. And I'm afraid I can't share client lists in any case, even if I knew who had purchased that particular item."

13

"You do know. I can tell. Look, I'm not a crazy stalker, I swear. I just want to talk to her."

"As all crazy stalkers have claimed since the beginning of time."

I let out a breath. She did have a point. "No, it's not like that. She kissed me. We kissed each other. You know that mistletoe at the gazebo?"

Kinleigh raised her ginger-colored eyebrows and waited.

"She was standing beneath it, and it was snowing, and God, she looked—"

"Willing to sleep with a handsome stranger who was a good kisser?"

"Obviously not, since I slept alone at the bed and breakfast." I frowned. "Did you just call me handsome? Pretty sure you're the only person who's said something nice to me since I drove into town. Except Dare, but you're a lot prettier than he is."

Wordlessly, she held up a hand and tapped her sparkly wedding ring.

I had to laugh. "I wasn't hitting on you. Just saying the welcome mat in this town has not been rolled out in my direction."

"Yet a beautiful woman kissed you thoroughly enough you're ready to search to the ends of the earth for her. Sounds pretty welcoming to me."

"So far, I've only been here. That's hardly searching to the ends of the earth."

"We get a lot of tourists for the winter festival."

"And she happened to have bought a scarf from you just before she met me?"

"Met you with her lips, you mean, since you haven't even said her name."

I had no answer for that.

"It's Christmas," I finally implored as her daughter released another cry from her white carriage a few feet away. Her mother's attention was obviously split, so I'd take advantage of any moment of weakness I could. She might not know I wasn't a serial killer but I did. "You have a baby and a husband. Or wife," I amended when she glanced back at me. "Surely you believe in romance."

"Making out under mistletoe is not necessarily romance, but okay, fine. How about this? I'll meet you halfway."

I waited.

"I'll contact her and let her know you're looking for her. If you leave your information with me, I'll pass it along if she's interested."

I frowned. "That's smart and very kind of you. Thank you for being so protective of your customers."

It was her turn to blink. "Are you warming up for her? I have to admit that's a good line."

I laughed as I scrawled my cell number on her mailing list signup pad and pushed it toward her. "Tell her my name is Callum. MacGregor," I added after a second. "I'm twenty-nine, single, and oh, I love vanilla ice cream. I'm staying in town a bit longer."

Mostly due to her, since my car would be ready in not too long. But I couldn't just walk—drive—away without making a real effort to find this woman.

Why? Because she has soft lips? Because she can kiss? Because her moan made you want to hear it when she was naked and on top of you?

I shifted uncomfortably, suddenly very thankful for my long coat. I hadn't expected to develop a semi in the middle of Kinleigh's vintage clothes and home goods shop, but Crescent Cove was turning out to be an experience in a number of ways.

"Maybe you should stop before the ice cream part," Kinleigh suggested, jotting down what I'd said just the same.

"She'll know what it means." Maybe, if I'd pegged her taste correctly.

"If you say so. Now if you'll excuse me..." She trailed off. "Luna, c'mere a sec."

A bouncy blond emerged from the back, jingling from her impressive collection of earrings and bracelets. "Sure thing, boss. What's up?"

Kinleigh unbuttoning her blouse was my cue to split. "Thanks again," I said before heading out. "Tell her to call day or night," I added just before I closed the door behind me.

Way to sound desperate.

I glanced up and down the block. I wasn't even certain I could recognize her in the daylight. Her hair had seemed pinkish in the dark. But I didn't know if it was straight or curly, since she'd had it in braids.

Hell, for all I knew, she'd run because she was dating someone. Or engaged. Or married. Maybe she'd done both of us a favor, and I'd just have to chalk it up to a good moment not meant to be repeated.

A *great* moment.

Feeling moronic, I wrapped the red scarf I still carried around my neck. Then I lifted the fringes to my nose and took a long sniff. Not even the faintest scent of vanilla. Nothing but cold, crisp air singeing off my nose hairs.

I didn't have a clue how to spend the day. My Christmas shopping for my family and Bryce and a few other friends had all been done before November 1st. I wasn't one for putting things off. But my mom might enjoy a trinket I found in one of the shops here.

Just give her the scarf. Pretty sure it's cashmere.

Nah, I'd just bide my time there.

I wandered in and out of a few shops. I found a kitten sun-catcher in one of them with a lake motif that I thought my mom might like in the dead of winter. A cat steering a boat was kind of weird, but she had a wacky enough sense of humor to appreciate it.

Then I took a walk near the water. Last night, I'd gotten a few clothes at a funky store called Vintage December so that I wouldn't have to wear the same outfit today and possibly tomorrow. Most of them were back at my room, but my messenger bag was still bulging from the sweater I'd brought with me for the day. The button-down was soft and a hell of a lot nicer than most of the things in my closet. I'd dropped a few hundred dollars in that shop since I hadn't exactly been prepared for an impromptu vacation in a lakeside town that had to be at least ten degrees colder than Syracuse.

After I shrugged on the cardigan, I closed my bag. The army green fabric was covered in old stamps in faded ink along with hand-sewn patches from all sorts of random cities in New York. I wondered if Crescent Cove had a patch I could add to my collection.

Maybe I'd have more interest in browsing later. For now, I was shopped out.

On my way back to the bed and breakfast, when I was shoulder to shoulder on the sidewalk with the midday shopping crowd—and yes, apparently the holiday festival was still in progress, judging from the amount of signs—I caught sight of a small art shop tucked beside the library. It was obviously new, and when I stepped inside, there were still dropcloths all over the floor.

"We aren't open yet, sorry," a woman on a stepladder called out.

Though it wasn't in my nature to be rude, I'd noticed two things I needed. I grabbed the sketch pad off an easel and plucked a hunk of charcoal out of a cup. "I have to have these. Name your price."

Her laugh was as airy as the windchimes tinkling from the eaves. "Well, seeing as you're my very first sale and I intend on framing that dollar, I won't overcharge you. But I'm really not open yet. I don't even have the register online."

"How's fifty bucks for you to frame?" I was already prying out my wallet. If I'd ever needed the supplies more, I couldn't remember it. "Extra because you're really helping me out of a jam with these."

"Sold." She held out a hand, and I gave her the money. Rings winked on every finger. "You're not spending your last dollar for those, are you? Here, let me get you a bag."

"No, I have a few left. Thanks." I let her take my purchases and put them in a paper sack before returning them to me. Then I slid my items into the messenger bag I'd grabbed from my car before turning it over to Dare.

True to her word, she slipped my money into a small frame she had waiting before hanging it on a hook on the wall. "There. Every Line A Story is officially in business. Thank you. I hope you'll come back when we're open for real in a couple weeks." She turned back and dusted her hand on her hip. "I'm Colette."

"Callum. Nice to meet you. Afraid I don't live here or travel this way, but I wish you all the luck."

She smiled, her long brown hair ponytail slipping over her shoulder. "If you change your mind, you know where to find me."

Inwardly, I sighed. If only I'd met her the day before. Now my head was full of possibly pink hair and unforgettably soft lips.

I nodded to her and went back outside, taking a bracing breath of the crisp, water-tinged air. At least the snow had stopped, although the slate gray sky warned it wouldn't be long.

We'd just see how long I would get.

I crossed the street and got lucky with a bench near the lake, just beyond the bulk of the festival mayhem. Even on the gloomy day, the small lapping waves of the lake glittered.

A giant snow globe had been set up near the shore. Fake snow whirled inside as children leaped around like little maniacs. I hoped the structure didn't take flight in the wind, but it seemed securely tethered.

If not, Sheriff Unfriendly would have something else to grouse about.

Christmas carols played brightly from unseen speakers, and the scent of real roasted chestnuts carried on the air. I drew in deeply and considered making a lunch of them—after I worked on my sketch.

I dug out my newest acquisitions from my bag and flipped to the first page in the pad. I skated my fingertips over the fine weave of the paper. It wasn't super high-end, but there was nothing like the promise of a fresh start.

Perhaps that was what Crescent Cove could be for me too. Even if I hadn't realized I was searching for one.

I started sketching the snow globe first to warm up my fingers, stiff from the cold. I rarely remembered to put on the gloves, which was a problem when stilted movements would affect the piece.

The shape took form quickly. I added in the snow now playfully meandering from the thick clouds above, an interesting juxtaposition to the world of faux flakes inside the dome. Kids tumbled over one another while their smiling parents lingered outside, talking and sipping cups of coffee or cocoa. I wondered if they'd laced them with something stronger. If those screeching children were mine, I'd probably imbibe before mid-afternoon too.

I swallowed over the sudden lump in my throat, moving my fingers faster to compensate. Coming from a large family myself, I'd never had the great desire to have kids. I'd grown up with the triplets climbing over everything that was nailed down—and some stuff that wasn't—and the idea of willingly filling my own quiet home with so much noise and activity was...

Not so bad. Not anymore.

I sat back on the bench and finished one of the kids' faces. I couldn't see that clearly from this distance, but I imagined her cheeks were flushed, and her long braids were bobbing over her shoulders.

Braids. Like my pink-haired mystery woman who might never be anything but that.

Quickly, I flipped the page and moved the charcoal in rapid strokes. I was guessing at her shape, especially in this stage of undress. In *any* stage of undress. Bulky winter coats could hide a lot. I didn't even know her true hair color or its texture.

But I had a good imagination.

She came together even faster than the snow globe. All sinuous lines and curves. A hint of fullness here and there. Rounded and then slight. Long hair trailing down her back like water, free and flowing. And that scarf still wrapped around my neck protecting her modesty—just barely. The soft material cupped her and teased at what she might reveal if the urge struck. Those tantalizing bits of fringe trailed along her inner thigh, caressing her flesh like a lover.

Or like a man driven to sketch her, since he might never see her again.

I spent the most time on her lips. Their perfect bow, the divot on the top one, the slight dent in the bottom. So plump and glossy and bitable. This was the only part of her I felt like I knew without question, though I wouldn't mind a lifetime to learn about the rest.

"Oh my God. What are you doing? Are you—is that—oh my God." At my side, a woman covered her mouth.

I blocked my sketch pad with my arm. This little town was driving me nuts. "It's my girlfriend," I said quickly. A lie, sure, but not entirely.

Fine, yes, entirely. One kiss—no matter how hot—did not a relationship make.

"Where is she?" the woman asked accusingly, glancing around. We were surrounded by some adults, but children were definitely more prevalent.

"I'm going to meet her now." I flipped the snow globe sketch over to cover the scarf one, although in retrospect, that might not have helped considering the subject of that one was kids. Which she noticed with a narrow-eyed stare the sheriff would have applauded. "I'm an artist," I muttered. "I've sold pieces. I have an agent."

"You aren't from Crescent Cove." Her statement whipped my skin with as much force as the snow-laden breeze. "Are you here for the festival?"

"I live in Syracuse." Defense and outrage laced my voice as I stood and shoved my supplies into my messenger bag. "I'm a professor, dammit."

"Mmm-hmm." She crossed her arms. "I'm friends with the sheriff, you know. So, you might just want to find your girlfriend," I half-expected her to do air quotes, "and move along."

Clearly, there was no point trying to explain myself. The woman in my sketch was quite obviously a fully grown woman, but maybe that also made me a pervert. The suggestion was there.

I'd been branded with a scarlet P in bucolic Crescent Cove.

With a quick salute, I crossed the snowy slope to the sidewalk. I was probably being a fool by sitting around and sketching as if the woman I sought would just fall into my lap.

Last night had been my chance, and I'd lost it. But maybe I would get a good commission out of the piece I'd just drawn, so it wasn't all bad.

I headed up the street, dodging dogwalkers and joggers and pedestrians toting a million shopping bags. It would be impossible soon to get through town. If Dare wasn't quite done with my car, it looked like I'd be spending the rest of the day in my room at the bed and breakfast. Ideally, I'd manage to dodge the far-too-nosy proprietress, Sage Hamilton, who had practically asked for my time of birth so she could run a report on me.

Seemed a common thing in this town.

I didn't get it. The place was crawling with tourists, and from what I'd seen with others, they seemed to be treated well. But something about me set off alarm bells or something. Not that Sage had been mean to me. Far from it. She'd acted as if she expected me to buy a home in town immediately, as if I'd fall under the Crescent Cove spell and never leave.

As if I could do nothing else.

I watched a couple embrace, the woman reaching up to cup the man's cheeks. Something about the moment pulled at me, and I knew I'd be sketching them later as well. The whole scene tugged at me. Her bright blue coat and her flushed cheeks and the snow swirling around them as he hauled her up off her feet so that she came half out of her impractical soft-soled shoes. She should have boots in this weather. The snow was piling up again, despite the heavy crowds clogging the sidewalk.

Everyone had somewhere to go. Someone to be with.

Except me.

I yanked out my phone. Maybe it was time I called Dare to nudge things along. At least I had some inspiration for my holiday break so I could spend time sketching around the family stuff, of which there would be plenty. My mom usually put up three or four trees and blasted Christmas music at levels typically reserved for teenagers.

And then I saw a flash of pink in the crowd.

Time stopped. My heart, my brain, and even my muscles went numb. Then I sprung into action.

Clutching my phone, I weaved through the festivalgoers, mumbling apologies, keeping my gaze firmly on my prize. She was moving quickly, but I was determined.

I just had to see if it was her. If it wasn't, I would give up and move on.

Somehow.

I surged forward and tapped the woman's shoulder. She looked back at me as hope briefly bloomed in my chest—

And it wasn't her. Not even close. Her face was all wrong. Her eyes were too close together, her lips were too thin. She smiled at me as I backed away, feeling like the most colossal idiot who had ever lived.

Until I turned my head and glimpsed the curvy woman standing in front of the café across the street.

Her hair wasn't pink. Wasn't even that light. At this distance, I could've mistaken her features. But I *knew* it was her.

Proving yet again I had no business in such an upstanding town, I dashed across the street outside the crosswalk. She didn't notice me as I jogged up to her, but that gave me time to study her face.

It was definitely her, and she was even more beautiful than I remembered. Even if now her hair was brown.

I unwound her scarf from around my neck, and her gaze shot to mine. "You lost this." I lifted the scarf. "And I'll return it, if you'll spend the rest of your life with me."

THREE

Ellie

THE AIR WAS BRISK, AND SNOW SNAPPED IN THE AIR. IT ALSO SWIRLED around the man I hadn't been able to get out of my mind for the last day.

Making out under the mistletoe wasn't exactly in my life plan. Then again, having three jobs kind of killed all ideas of romance. So much so that the kiss seemed like a fuzzy flash in a dream. The kind you wake from with a gasp and can't quite shake.

Because surely that didn't happen in real life to a woman like me.

It happened in those Hallmark movies I secretly binge-watched in July and November through December. I couldn't help it. Those happy hours were a soft paintbrush over my usual lonely Christmases. Add in the Polaroids I took of styles for my look book, and watching those movies was almost like homework in between the moments of longing.

But it wasn't real.

And neither was getting kissed by a stranger.

Even if this stranger had stunning gray eyes that matched the perpetually overcast sky of my hometown. Intelligence sparked there and made all sorts of crazy thoughts flutter in my brain like the flakes that spun around on the shelf of snow globes that lined my bedroom bookcase.

And because I wanted to step closer to him, I folded my arms over my bulging look book journal against my chest. He was holding my favorite cashmere scarf. The one I'd bought myself for graduation. Okay, so cosmetology school wasn't exactly like a college graduation, but I had a brand spanking new certificate that said I could cut hair in the state of New York. For me, that was a big thing. It had warranted a rare splurge of spending on myself.

His long, slightly dirty fingers were holding out the scarf to me like a gift. Well, it wasn't quite dirt on them, but they sure weren't clean.

I glanced down at those fingers and quickly tucked the urge to snarl at him that he was ruining the fine fabric under the polite smile I pasted on my face. "Forever shouldn't be offered up so easily for a scrap of cashmere."

He brought the crimson scarf up to his whiskered chin and slid it down his neck. "It's a lovely scrap of cashmere, and I wish I could say it still smells like you." He inhaled and something warm and foreign unfurled in my belly. "Unfortunately, that's not the case. But I remember how you tasted. And that's why vanilla is my new favorite flavor until the end of time."

I narrowed my eyes. "Then go to The Rusty Spoon and have yourself a vanilla milkshake. I highly recommend it."

A flash of teeth gleamed from his full lips. He had just enough scruff to make my palms itch to touch, and a head of thick hair that the hairdresser flourishing inside of me wanted to get a hold of. But it was the lonely woman inside of me who was the real troublemaker. She wanted to step closer and see if that kiss was just a fluke.

But she was me, and that wasn't happening.

"Then come with me."

"What?" I blinked out of the haze that seemed to descend when I was with him. "No. I have to work."

"Then after work."

I shook myself out of the stupor. "I don't know you. I don't go out with strangers."

He held out his hand. "Callum MacGregor."

Of course he had a hot name. Hell, it was a Hallmark movie name. Not a real guy. Not a George or Gary or Greg. Nope, he was a Callum.

I glanced down at his hand, but I didn't take it. I only hugged my notebook tighter. "Look, I'm flattered. And that kiss was…"

"Amazing. Stupendous. Life-altering."

I frowned. "It was a kiss."

He stepped forward. "You felt it. I know you did. You pulled me closer." His attention dropped to my mouth, and he reached for me.

I stepped back, my spine going rigid. "It was stupid."

His eyebrows snapped down. "No it wasn't. It was the best thing that has happened to me in a damn long time."

"Then you need some new hobbies."

"I have plenty of hobbies, thanks. More than I can keep up with. What I don't have is your name."

I took another step back and slammed into the handle of the door to Brewed Awakening. Flustered, I dropped my notebook, and he swooped down to pick it up before the snow soaked into the pages.

"Hey. Give that back."

He took my arm and gently moved me aside as a trio of girls came out with their coffees cupped in their hands as they talked animatedly about some guy from a TV show. I smiled at them awkwardly. They were regulars in the café.

The shorter one of the three glanced at me and then at my hot mistake, tilting her head with interest. "Who's your friend, Ellie?"

I resisted the urge to growl at Katie. Now he knew my name.

"Ellie, is it? It suits you." His long, dusty fingers clutched my idea book easily. As if they were born for such things. Long fingers that had cupped my face so tenderly, though they'd been much cleaner then. Hygiene was important, dammit.

I reached for my notebook again, and he held it just out of reach. "He's no one. Stranger danger."

Katie's demeanor changed in a second. All three girls advanced on him. "Is he bothering you?"

Callum held up his other hand. "No trouble. Just trying to get to know the woman I'm going marry."

Katie's sky blue eyes went shiny. "Marry?" She curled her fingers around her to-go cup and brought it up for a quick sip, foam teasing her top lip. "Like love at first sight?"

"Oh, for God's sake. Keep the book and my favorite freaking scarf for all I care." I rushed around the girls and grabbed the door handle. "I'm going to be late, and Macy will kill me."

"Excuse me, ladies," Callum said with that charming drip of honey voice before he followed me inside. "C'mon, I'm harmless. There was an instant connection between us. You felt it too, or you wouldn't be so pissed at me."

I shrugged out of my coat. Before I could get it all the way down my long-sleeved uniform shirt, he was there to help. I huffed out an annoyed breath even as his snow-tinged cedar scent slid around me. The same scent that had chased me into dreams last night. My skin prickled where his calloused fingers grazed my wrist.

He draped my coat over his arm, and I did growl this time. "I don't have time for this."

"I'll hold onto it until your shift is over." He tucked my look book into the messenger bag over his shoulder. "It'll be safe with me. Same as you, Ellie. I promise."

"That's what murderers say."

His eyebrow spiked. "You know a few murderers?"

"No, but I watch plenty of true crime shows. Ted Bundy was super charming, wasn't he?"

"Not really. If you looked closer, his eyes were dead. Any woman with half a bit of awareness would see the same. You are far too wary to get tricked like that."

Tell that to my last boyfriend who got me to pay for half of the things he called essentials that he was short on cash for. Like his cell phone service and that nifty iPad I got him for Christmas last year.

I narrowed my eyes. "Or you're charming enough to tell stories like that to make a woman feel safe."

His hand darted out to circle my wrist. His gray eyes went dark in reaction. "I feel your pulse skittering. You feel this *thing* between us too."

"Could just be fear."

"Not of me. I'm harmless, unlike my triplet brothers. They're hell on earth." He pulled on the lapel of his sweater. "Would a serial killer wear a cardigan?"

Probably not and no one should look so good in that stupid brown sweater, but he did. "Maybe a smart one would. You seem like a smart guy. Maybe too smart for your own good."

"That's what my mom tells me." His long lashes swept down as he focused on my mouth again. "And I will say I'm smart enough not to let you get away again." Then his gaze crashed into mine once more. "Not without examining just what's between us."

"You're not from Crescent Cove or you'd be running for the hills, buddy. There's no dating in the Cove. There's only forever and so many babies you could rename us Bunny Cove."

There. That should send him running. Most men who were smart and under thirty-ish escaped while they still could.

I couldn't quite tell his age. There were lovely crinkles at the corners of his eyes, but that could just mean he liked to be outside.

Dammit, I needed to stop staring at him.

He swallowed tightly, and the flare of fear that he'd vanish just like I thought was quickly banked.

Or maybe I was afraid he'd stay. I couldn't decide which one was scarier.

He slid his fingers down my hand to tangle with my fingers. "That just makes me want to hear more."

"No, you don't. You want to turn right around and head back to wherever you come from."

"Wrong." The corner of his mouth lifted. "I'm actually trapped here until my car is done."

"I—"

"Yo, Vanilla, I'm pretty sure my schedule still has your name on it."

My shoulders rose to my ears at Macy Gideon's shout. She was my boss for a little while longer. However, she'd used my order nickname so I wasn't in real trouble.

I shook him free and pointed at him. "If you leave with my notebook, I'll find you and chop off those dirty fingers."

He laughed and looked down at his hand. "Sorry, I was sketching in the park."

Of course he was an artist. If there was a guy who was ill-equipped to be an adult, I was going to be attracted to him. Not this time. I was going to be strong and not fall for someone who had *no future* stamped on his forehead.

I turned to head into the back of the café where a line of people were waiting to be served. I hurried to the cash register and quickly tapped in my login, and then grabbed an apron from the drawer and tugged it over my head.

"Where do you need me?"

Macy's short hair was in frazzled spikes, telling me it had been a day already. She had three espresso pods brewing in the big purple beast that dominated the side counter. "Need a new batch of coffee in the carafes."

"Got it." I turned to the long counter and pulled off the magnetic timers and reset them for another three hours. Habit and auto pilot took over, even while Callum's intrusive personality vied for space in my too busy brain. I hooked the long handles over my arm and gathered all four thermoses up and then headed to the kitchen to use the industrial-sized brewer.

I'd been working at the café since Macy opened it a few years ago. She paid well, and I could always pick up a shift when I wanted extra cash. Now she had a much larger staff, but I was one of the originals, so I always got first pick of the bonus shifts. I was also the one everyone called because I could never say no to adding more money to my savings account.

But all that was going to change.

My cosmetology certificate was finally going to let me move on the plans I'd been making for the last four years. My bulging notebook and Pinterest board would finally have an outlet. I didn't have to only be the girl who washed hair and swept up clippings just to soak up real life experience at To Dye For, the new salon that had opened this year. I officially had my own booth rental as of Monday.

I would be hanging up my apron Monday after the morning shift and trading it for a smock—a really cute black one with pink Christmas trees on it—and a closetful of clothes I'd slowly been gathering to show off my true style. Not the jeans and array of café and pizza T-shirts that I wore most of the time.

The real me.

Would he be interested in that girl?

Ugh. No. I wasn't interested in starting some fling with Mr. Charming.

I touched my lips. They still buzzed at the thought of him. Life was changing for the better, and there was no room for a hot artist with clever lips in my current plans.

Even if I almost wished there was.

FOUR

Ellie

SIX HOURS LATER, MY ARTIST SHADOW HAD MOVED FROM THE MAIN CAFÉ to the the well-worn leather couch in the reading nook. He'd been busily scratching in his sketchbook, his gaze tracking my movements off and on. Just enough off that I didn't call Sheriff Brooks. Stalking wasn't sexy.

Callum, however, didn't give off that creepy vibe. He was just intense.

Along with being charming, he could make small talk with anyone and everyone. It was an enviable trait, but it still pissed me off. Especially since every female seemed to fall under his spell.

Including Mrs. Gunderson who could talk a body into the ground and then shovel after them to talk some more. But he didn't look bothered in the least.

I shot a glance over my shoulder at the chirpy laugh that came out of the older woman. Dear God, was she flirting with him?

Callum caught me looking and gave me a half smile that made every blood cell in my system go into overdrive before he refocused that obscene attention on Judy. There was no annoyance in his eyes, just a quiet friendliness that seemed to draw everyone into his sphere.

A few murmurs of gossip had fluttered through the air the first hour.

That he was trouble and had been sketching in the park—what kind of man was he?

By the end of the lunch rush, he had a line of people waiting for portraits.

He didn't charge, so Macy didn't give him any trouble as long as he kept buying food and drinks. I'd also spotted him stuffing twenties into the tip jar at the register every time he got a coffee or tea. Was he trying to buy me off?

What kind of woman did he think I was?

Annoyed, I marched over to pick up the dishes scattered around him. A cookie plate with a few crumbs was stacked on his panini plate, and there was now a collection of mugs. I went around the back of the couch he'd made his mini office and literally couldn't go another step.

On his pad was a perfect rendering of the book nook area, including the haphazard mix of Halloween and Christmas that was Macy's aesthetic. From the perspective to the tiny details it was like a photograph, only far more clever. He'd added a few faces on the pink pumpkins stacked everywhere. Some were sweet, some reminded me of *The Nightmare Before Christmas*, and still others had a flair that was completely his own.

In the center of the portrait was Macy's step-daughter, Dani, who was in her usual spot doing homework. Instead of her face in a book, he'd created a rendering of her climbing the bookcase in the midst of decorating the top shelf. She had a sweetly mischievous look on her face and a lock of hair falling forward from her sharp pixie cut that matched Macy's.

"That's amazing."

I wanted to saw off my tongue. Giving him compliments would not move him along in any way.

Mrs. Gunderson shifted and looked over the top of the couch at me. "Isn't he amazing? I've commissioned him to do my cats for Christmas."

I pressed my lips together against a laugh. When it was sufficiently buried, I stepped around the end table and gathered his plates. "Is that right?"

Callum grinned. "They sound like rapscallions."

Judy's laughter filled the room. "Oh, you are so correct. I can't wait. Are you sure that forty dollars is enough? It seems like your talent is worth so much more."

He patted Judy's hand. "Well, I'm here for a bit longer it seems." The look he gave me could have melted my panties. "It keeps my skills sharp."

"If they get any sharper, you'll need to open up your own shop," I muttered.

"Would you like that? Me here all the time?" He curled his long fingers around the handle of his mug and brought it to his lips. "Seeing you everyday would definitely make work far more palatable. I even got my own drink from Macy."

"What?" I blinked and my hand stilled over the stack of mugs. "She gave you one?"

He grinned. "Is that something special? I had a feeling it was kind of her thing."

"Yeah, but only if she likes you. And it usually takes at least five or six visits before she gives someone their own drink."

"I didn't have a choice in the drink. She just put it in front of me."

"That's how it works."

"Hmm." He took another sip. "Now she calls me Bourbon."

"Wow." Her bourbon-aged espresso beans weren't pulled out very often. Then again, he had been stuffing big bills into the tip jar. Macy was often a slave to the almighty dollar. Charging him extra for her special blend plus all those tips… Well, how could she resist?

Especially since he was obviously a city boy of some sort. He probably wouldn't notice the difference in cost.

Callum nodded to another coffee sitting just behind his stack. "That's yours if you'd like to quench your thirst."

I glanced down at the coffee. *My* coffee. It wasn't terribly original, but when it came to Macy's strong brew, I needed the sweetness of vanilla and milk with a dash of honey. Honey being her secret ingredient for me. It had taken two years for her to tell me what it was.

"Why did you get my drink?"

"For you, of course."

"I'm working."

"You work in a café. I'm pretty sure you're going to drink the product sometime."

I gathered the cups. "I'm fine."

"Suit yourself," he called after me.

I picked up the pace and dumped the mugs in my bin and brought it all into the back. Macy was waiting there for me.

"So, what's the story?"

"There isn't a story." I moved to the dishwasher and started stacking mugs and cups into the correct slots.

"Oh, there's a story. He's been sniffing after you for hours now."

"Right. It's been awhile. Shouldn't you be heading home anyway? You never stay away from Michael this long."

"He's with Grumps for the afternoon. Don't change the subject."

I gripped the edge of the counter. "I don't know why he's still here."

"*Zzzt*. Try again."

I huffed out a breath. "It's stupid, and he's just being stubborn. He'll go away soon."

"Considering he's spent about eighty bucks here, not including those big tips—I don't think so."

"Eighty? What are you charging him?"

Macy shrugged. "He keeps buying for all the people who sit for his pretty pictures."

"What did Dani get out of him?"

"Double chocolate chip cookies and hot chocolate." Macy gave me a wolfish smile. "She knows how to play men. I feel that I'll be in trouble in about five years."

I laughed despite my own annoyance. "I think you're right. You'll have too much fun needling Gideon."

Her grin widened. "I live for making my husband nuts."

"What's that like?"

She frowned. "You know Gideon."

"I know." I shook my head. "Never mind."

"Uh-oh. Are you drinking the Cove Kool-Aid?"

"No. Well, maybe a little. I'm in no rush for the baby part, but I'm tired of the dating roulette wheel. I'd like a guy who isn't into games." I peeked out into the dining room. I could just glimpse Callum on the couch. "He's got games stamped all over him."

"Even in the granddad sweater?"

I let the door close. "Not sure I've ever seen a grandfather fill out the shoulders of a sweater like that."

"So, you have been looking. I knew there was a story. I can always smell it."

"Your nose should be singed from coffee."

"Blaspheme."

I laughed as I crossed my arms and leaned against the counter. "We had a stupid moment under the mistletoe at the festival last night. It was snowing and the twinkle lights were bright and there he was all chilled and out of place. Rosy nose and funnel cake powder on his coat. Then he just sort of…"

"Planted one on you?"

"Ugh." I could feel the heat flooding my neck and cheeks. "Yes. I wasn't expecting it, and he actually knows how to kiss—which is kind of a miracle compared to a lot of guys out there."

"That's a fact. Kinda how Gideon and I got into trouble. Though I was the one planting one on him."

"On camera."

Macy rolled her eyes. "Yeah, let's not talk about that. Especially since it wasn't the first time. Look, there's no harm in finding out how it might go between you. I mean, he's not from the Cove so maybe he isn't afflicted like the rest of them. Just you know, wrap it twice."

"Macy." I twisted the end of my ponytail and wrinkled my nose.

"What? It's true. Then again, we've had a few strangers wander through, and they still end up planting babies in unsuspecting women of this town. Maybe you're right. Don't hook up with the hot artist dude."

"Right. See? That's the smart thing."

"Smart thing. Yep. You're a smart girl."

"I am." I nodded. "See, you're good at this stuff."

"But…"

I tipped back my head. "No buts."

"First of all—no, this is definitely not my bag. However, you not going to be under my daily watch anymore."

"I'll only be a few storefronts down. I'm not moving to Syracuse or anything."

"Still."

I grinned at her. "Maybe you'll even let me cut your hair."

She narrowed her eyes at me. "I do okay."

I sighed. So much for Macy as my first paid customer. "That's true. Someone must have taught you how to cut."

She shrugged. "My mom was a hairdresser. It's not an easy life. Then again, you're used to being on your feet all day anyway. And I have a feeling you'll be just fine."

My eyes burned. "You think?"

"As I said, you're smart. You don't trip over your tongue because a hot dude smiles at you like a lot of the baristas who have worked here. If he gets your blood pumping, maybe don't shut him down right away. You can go on a date like normal people."

"I'm starting a new job."

"Right. *A* job—not three like you have been doing. Just one job, like the rest of us."

"You have two jobs."

She waved me away. "I don't count. I like both my jobs."

"I love my job here."

"No. You are very competent at your job and I appreciate that. But this isn't your passion. I see you ripping pages out of the magazines left in the book nook."

I flushed. "I'm sorry."

"It's fine. I don't care. I'm aware that people in town just like to dump their magazines on me from their kids' school magazine drives. But I see your brain spinning, and then you're off stealing my tape dispenser to play collage with your idea book."

I winced.

She pulled out a little Moleskine notebook from her back pocket. "I have one too." She shoved it back in her pocket. "It's in code, so don't think you can steal my secrets."

"Apparently not, Al!" shouted Sal back.

"We could still get my guy here ya know," said Grandpa, still calm, and sitting with his hands folded on the kitchen table.

"No offense, Pop," started Sal, "but your guy is probably older than you."

Before Grandpa could react, Al instinctively backed his brother's opinion, "Yeah Pop, let's be realistic here."

"I can still kick both your asses!" yelled their father, sending the two a few steps back.

"Vincent! Your pressure," Grandma reminded.

Sal began to lose his macho demeanor now that his mother had become visibly upset. Whenever Sal lost his cool he began to talk to himself; "I knew it, I told you, stick with the plan, just like Pop taught us, stick to the plan and everything works out..."

"Plan!" Stella winced as she heard the word come out of her own mouth. "You bums! What are you up to!"

"What plan!" Al shouted back, feigning ignorance, "He meant we should have stuck with the kid's pick, that's all!"

"They're up to something, Stella," Grandma whispered to her only daughter.

"Ma, c'mon," pleaded Al, "The kid checked his pick's background better than the FBI could, that's all he meant, c'mon Ma, don't be upset. There was no camera. I'm making cannoli today. Dairy free, for the kid."

"Whatevah..." Stella finished, with a cold disapproving glare. "I know they're up to something Ma."

While they argued upstairs Han turned the lights down in his private space and lay back on the floor. He was suddenly tired, and felt like he might cry. He wanted to get up, go to the refrigerator, and get his injection, but fatigue was overtaking him. He closed his eyes and tried to rest. Who was that weird lady he wondered, and how long until Aeson gets here?

———

Katie Carouche exceeded the speed limit. She hurled her car into a turn at close to 100 mph. She closed her eyes, let go of the wheel, and allowed the car's computer to take over. The bright vehicle spun and the safety sensors took over, righted the sports car, and avoided even a scratch. It came to a standstill and Carouche sat in darkness. The center console lit up with text and she opened her eyes.

What happened? Did you get the job? Did you see him?

Carouche looked into the green screen and tapped out her reply on the keyboard above the emergency brake.

It didn't go as planned. He didn't show himself. I'm sorry.

The console's glow became irritating to look at and Carouche began to chew on the knuckles of her right hand. When she felt her boss was finished and that there would be no more communication she took hold of the screen and turned it around. The back of the console was well padded and had the marks of use. She started the ignition, got on the road, and punched the makiwara training board with her right fist as she drove with her left. Her foot lay heavy on the pedal and her punches got harder and harder.

———

"No phone huh?" the tall skinny man asked.

"It's dead, I think the lady who..." Aeson began to explain.

"We don't use phones either, radiation, messes with the chi," he stated, licking his gums for the remnants of the pill that he pulverized with his teeth. "But I know where we could get one."

"I really need to make a call. Can you at least tell me if there are any public phones around?" the fighter, beginning to despair, pleaded.

"Hmmmm..." the lady said, still breathing heavily, "you could buy a disposable, but ain't no store's around here. Stores don't last long round here. We know somebody with a phone though."

Someone shouted at them from across the street; "Hey! Junkies! You gonna introduce us to your little white friend?"

Aeson pocketed the pills and put one hand on his backpack. What's next, he wondered. And how am I ever going to get to Alpine?

———

Han dreamed the sweet animal dreams that his injections often stifled. He floated within a green canopy, and soft primal sounds came out of his mouth. A food patch presented itself. Multi colored fruit hung before him and he heard himself squeal in delight.

"Hey kid! You want me to get you something to eat? Your guys gonna be here soon ya know," Uncle Al let Han know without barging in on him.

"Yeee! Yeee! Wyeeeyah!" Han sounded off as he rose from sleep, surprising himself when he heard his dream's voice in the waking world.

"Han! You OK?" Al asked as he slid the glass door open.

Han rubbed his eyes and yawned, then looked at Uncle Al. Han tilted his head slowly without breaking his gaze. It was as if he didn't recognize his uncle anymore.

"Kid? What are you up to?"

Han's eyes grew more intense as they drank in the world, and his lips curled upward as much as they could curl to become an excited and mischievous smile. "Yeeee! Yeeee!" he screeched out, showing the entirety of his teeth and throat.

"Sal! Get down here!" Al commanded while turning towards the main room. Al knew that he needed to get to the small refrigerator behind the bar before his nephew could.

Han was too fast, and too long without his weekly gene therapy injection. Before Al knew it he was standing in a very dark room. Han locked the door with his palm's signature, leaving Al to stumble around for the exit.

The now wide awake twelve year old howled again, tremendously pleased with his first act of rascality. "Yeee! Yeee!"

In a single leap Han was on top of the pool table, from there he bounced to the bar and removed the already full syringe. Before Al could get his cell phone out to warn the others Han was already rolling out onto the kitchen's floor. He screamed laughingly with all his might.

"What's next?" Aeson asked himself cautiously.

"What's next is give us the rest of those tasty treats and we'll have no trouble," said the squat, drug starved lady.

"Couple more treats like Lulu said and we'll cover your ass," spoke the man, who seemed less jittery but still full of the hunger.

"Tasty treats! What you dealing in our hood cracker!" shouted a raspy voice from behind a high leather collar. He had five cohorts with him, and by the time Aeson stood up they were already surrounding him.

"I'm not dealing anything. I'm just waiting for a bus," Aeson let them know with his returned calm demeanor.

"Well, you'll be waiting a long time, cuz the next bus that stops here is tomorrow morning. Now! String Bean and Rice Ball, what did he give you!"

"Synthoazapine," the homeless couple answered in chorus.

"Really? My word. Big pharma has arrived," the threatening man commented facetiously.

Aeson heard knuckles popping and limbs warming up beneath leather and denim. They were about to start swinging. Aeson wondered to himself if more than one of them would break their hand on his head. He knew at least the first guy to throw a punch would suffer.

Something must have come over the tall lanky drug addicted man. A memory of a nobler time came upon him perhaps, and for a moment, he became his former self; "We were just researching our own experiences, Walter, that's all, this guy's not dealing, we just…"

"Maybe I'll see you tomorrow." I'd suddenly developed more interest in sticking around town, so the possibility was there.

"Maybe I'll beat you at drawing again."

I laughed. "Wouldn't doubt it."

I tucked my supplies into my messenger bag. If I stuck around, I was going to have to stop into Colette's place again. I was about two-thirds of the way through the hundred-page sketchbook just from sitting here for a day. And while some of the pieces were throwaway warmup sketches, a lot of them were actually good studies that just might be something more.

I was all about using models when I needed to, but for the most part, I preferred everyday subjects and Crescent Cove was full of characters. From the nosy busybody types, to the prolific level of children, and the added strangers in town for the festival, I'd been inundated with subject matter. People from all walks of life came in and out of the café. Some I drew from mental snapshots, while others were curious enough to ask to sit for me.

My brain was whirling with ideas for a new series, which my agent would be super excited about considering I'd been dry for the last few months. The fall term always sucked all the creativity out of me. All that new hope wrapped in the careless throwaway years of youth. I reached a few students—enough to keep my own hope alive. Occasionally, I found little pockets of inspiration within our class discussions. Some students even surprised me with their takes on old folklore.

The winter term was more for my advanced classes. They were wrapped up in their own projects, and that often gave me time to deal with my own. As well as allowing me to get my annual book published to keep my place at the college. If you didn't publish, you perished. At least that was the current dean's point of view.

I had my initial research done on Tam Lin, a Scottish folktale. I was actually toying with writing an illustrated book. The prospect was scary as hell. I liked the anonymity of my alter ego, Cal. No last name on my paintings, just a sliced up version of my first. It was too unusual to use the full version without someone being able to connect a few dots.

At the very least, my Crescent Cove sojourn had produced enough seeds for a half dozen paintings. Dry period be gone.

For once, everything was falling in line. I should be settled, but instead, it was as if the whole world was a little tilted. I had a feeling that was more from a certain smart-mouthed barista.

One who had disappeared in the last hour or so.

I felt around in my bag and found her heavy notebook. It was bulging with clippings and glued-in notes. I didn't mean to open it. I knew more than most how much a sketchbook was more like a personal journal. But the spine was practically cracked with all the extra papers that had been added.

Glossy magazine pages had been ripped and altered, largely of women's faces and hair. Some had been restructured with pencils and paints while others had literally been cut to create a different style.

Notes were scribbled in the margins, numbers and names that didn't make a lick of sense to me.

A few brand names that I vaguely understood were highlighted with phone numbers or ID numbers—I couldn't tell which. But it was her script handwriting I was more interested in. It was slashing and feminine, not the cutesy teen bubble-style. No, this was the kind that came with a quick brain who couldn't get the words out fast enough.

Some of it had to be her own brand of shorthand.

I kept turning the pages. Her sense of color was startlingly intense. From the rich browns and reds to a million shades in between. It took a special eye to see variations like she did. And the way she hacked at photos to create her own hairstyles then moved on to scratchy drawings that refined them into faceless drawings that reminded me of fashion drawings.

But she didn't seem to care about clothing, so I was more inclined to think she was into the cosmetology end of art.

"Nosy much?"

I snapped the book shut and looked up. "Sorry, it sort of..." I stood and was pretty sure my tongue rolled out of my head and across the café to stop at her feet.

She'd changed.

The sweet ponytail had been replaced with a tumble of light brown waves tinged with caramel. Large gold hoops hung from her ears and she'd done something with her face. It was enhanced with some female witchcraft. Not the kind that looked overdone. No, this was the little tricks of her trade, now that I knew her a little better.

She'd changed into some sort of dusky pink sweater that looked cloud soft and slipped off one shoulder—I intended to find out just how soft it was, mind you. Of course then there was the skin tight white jeans and boots that matched her sweater. But not just a regular pair of boots. These went over her knee with a spiked heel that made her legs look miles long.

Fuck.

"Sort of what? Hopped out of your bag and into your hand and the pages magically fanned open?" She crossed her arms, and it did ridiculous things to the curve of her chest. Also, her sweater lifted the tiniest bit to show off a slash of golden stomach.

Was she wearing a bra?

There was definitely no strap going on there. Maybe it was one of those strapless things that only women understood. Or just one strap? I didn't understand, but I wanted to. And I really wanted it to be on my floor tonight. Or just the sweater. I wasn't choosy. I just wanted her.

"Uh…"

"Eyes up, pal."

I blew out a breath. "Sorry. You…wow."

Her lips quirked up at the corner. Damn, she knew her power. Why did that make her even hotter?

I cleared my throat. "I was looking for you and then I took out the notebook and it was ready to bust open."

She dropped her arms and came for me. I mean, came forward. The slow roll of her hips and those legs of hers made me crazy. I couldn't form a fucking thought. She tipped her head slightly and the scent of vanilla and honey flooded my senses. From the dusting of something shimmery on her shoulder to the glimmer of gold at her neck, ears, and wrists, she sparkled. She was a winter dream right in front of me.

And I was totally botching this. Again.

She took the notebook and dropped it into the huge bag over her other shoulder. "Thanks for keeping it safe. *Ish.*"

"I didn't touch it. Well, I mean I looked at a few pages, but I didn't hurt anything. It's really amazing," I finished lamely.

"Thanks. I've been collecting for a long time."

"Just collecting?"

She stepped closer. "Guess I'll find out Monday."

"What's Monday?"

"Do you really care, Callum?"

"Of course I do."

"You'll be gone by then, won't you?" She tipped her head and tucked a heavy lock of hair behind her ear. "Better question is why are you still here?"

"We had a moment."

"Yeah. It was a moment. A nice one."

"It was more than nice and you know it." I stepped into her space and some of her bravado seemed to fall away.

She shrugged. "I'm not looking for a bit of mistletoe-flavored fun, Callum. Come to think of it, it's poisonous. Did you know that?"

"I did. And actually in Norse mythology, it was the single thing that killed Baldr. He was immune to everything thanks to his mother, Frigg. Save for one little plant." I invaded her space. "An arrow made of mistletoe was his ultimate demise."

She licked her lips and stared at my mouth. "I didn't know that part."

"Then again, there were the Druids who used mistletoe in a lot of their rituals. They thought it had special powers. And as most things in pagan religion, the Christians nicked it for their own." I slid my fingers along her hip. "It went from being used in solstice rituals with evergreen for various fertility reasons to finally becoming little pretty things in doorways and arches to catch a kiss."

There were a lot more stories around mistletoe, but right now, most of it was leaving my brain. Probably because most of my blood had headed south.

"Oh."

Her lashes swept down and I went for it once again. Instead of the bite of winter and snow with traces of vanilla, she tasted of sharp mint. But her sigh was the same, and when she melted into me, I took full advantage. I wrapped my arm around her back and drew her up against me.

The café sounds fell away, and there was nothing but her honey-scented sweetness. I resisted the urge to break a few laws—sex in public was definitely frowned upon, especially in a small town. And I'd already made that colossal mistake with our intimate public moment.

Instead, I tempered myself into a long, slow kiss. She gripped my shirt, and I was pretty sure a few chest hairs were sacrificed for the cause. I didn't care. She was with me now, and that was all that mattered.

SIX

Ellie

FOR THE SECOND TIME IN AS MANY DAYS, I FOUND MYSELF KISSING THIS man. And as with the first kiss, I didn't really understand why it happened. Only that I liked it.

A lot.

At least the first one I could blame on mistletoe. This one? Not so much.

The crash of dishes behind me finally dented the hormone haze. Callum being an artist and spouting random stories about mistletoe shouldn't have been a turn-on, and yet here I was.

I stepped back and teetered on my heels. He caught me and the very sizable hardness he was sporting should have put me off, and yet it so did not.

Those words *and yet* were my problem tonight.

Everything about him should have been in my turn-off column. No roots in Crescent Cove—check. Less than stable artist—check. Not looking for something serious—double check.

And here I was, dressed up and looking to impress.

Run, Eleanor Ann Lawton, you run right now.

Not toward him. Away.

Ignoring that voice, I leaned in and brushed his lips one more time. "Let's make this mistake worth it."

He frowned. "Why does it have to be a mistake?"

"You don't exactly have *let's date* in mind, do you?"

"I could." He looked away too fast.

"Yeah, that's what I thought."

"I don't know what this is yet. I do know I want to spend time with you."

I readjusted my purse on my arm. "You want to spend time in my bed."

"Well, I'm not averse to that, no."

The fact that I wasn't either gave me a lot of pause. I'd never been the kind of woman who hopped into bed with strangers. I usually ended up having shit taste in men, but it took a while to figure that out. And that usually included five dates or so. "You're not from here, either."

"No." His eyes narrowed. "Why do I have a feeling you are going down a list in your head, and I'm not getting any checkmarks?"

"I have a lot of plans, Callum."

"Say it again, Ellie."

Something fluttered deep in parts of me I didn't want to think about. "I have a lot of plans."

"Callum. Say my name, Ellie."

"Stop being charming."

He grinned. "Well, there's one checkmark."

"Charming isn't a virtue."

"Is that what you're looking for? Virtues?" His gaze dropped to my mouth again as he rolled his bottom lip behind his teeth. And that was far too enticing. "Virtues don't keep you warm at night."

"I don't need a man to keep me warm at night. I've been taking care of myself for a damn long time. I even pay my own heating bill."

"That little bite in your voice doesn't do anything to turn me off, Ellie. It just makes me want you more."

"You have some weird standards."

"I'm pretty sure it's just an Ellie standard. You're ruining me for all other women, remember?"

"That endless charm is going to get you into trouble."

"I don't really have a lot of charm for anyone but you."

"Oh, I witnessed plenty of it during my shift today."

"You *were* paying attention."

I tossed my hair over my shoulder. "I didn't have to. The crowd around you told the tale no matter where I was in the café."

"Ah, but you still looked for me."

I huffed out a breath. "You are incorrigible."

"So my mother tells me. She'd like you."

My gut twisted. I didn't want to think about his family or the three brothers he'd mentioned. It seemed big and intrusive and...warm. I was used to my solitary life. I had a few friends, but somehow I'd never really gotten too close to anyone in the years I'd lived here. My mom had landed here when I was seventeen. By the time I was eighteen, she'd lit out with bum number twenty-three and left me behind. Not that she'd ever really been a mom. But once I was eighteen, she didn't have to legally stick around anymore.

"Hey." He slid his fingers into my hair and brushed his thumb over my cheek. "Where did you go?"

"Nowhere fun." I brushed his hand away.

"I'm just asking for you to give me tonight. If you still think this is a mistake after that, no harm no foul."

"What's the point? You don't even live around here."

"But I'm not far from here either. Less than an hour."

I sighed. "Might as well be five. I'm starting a new job on Monday, and I won't have time for two-hour long booty calls. And that's hoping it would be more than fifteen minutes."

"Oh, it would be. Not sure I can go two hours, but I'll give it a go."

I arched my brow.

He frowned then tipped his head back. "Oh, you mean to and from."

"Exactly." I toyed with the buttons of his goldenrod and soot colored shirt. The plaid suited him. A little traditional, but somehow not. His gray eyes were darker now. Stormier and intense in a way that made me want to make those mistakes. To throw caution out the window and live a little.

Especially with that lure of more than a fifteen-minute one and done.

No. No, that's not on the menu.

We could have a nice evening together without sex. It would be easier to walk away if I didn't know exactly how we fit together. Some fun might be good for me.

Hmm, how much longer than fifteen minutes would be take?

"Isn't it exhausting to think so much?" He played with the hem of my sweater, the backs of his knuckles brushing along the skin of my midriff. "Just jump in with me. Just for a few hours."

I sighed. I really was tired of thinking all the time. "Gonna buy me a steak?"

"Is that what you want?"

I laughed. "Macy said I should make you buy me an expensive dinner."

"I'd do it if that's what you want." He trailed his fingers over my hip to get to my hand and laced our fingers. "What do you want, Ellie?"

I let myself consider the possibilities. "I'd like to walk around the festival. I'm usually working and never get to enjoy it."

"Then that's what we'll do." He drew me closer to the couch and grabbed my coat. "Now aren't you glad I had your coat?"

"Is that what we're going to call it? And not ransom?"

"I'll do what I have to so I can spend time with you." He twirled me around. "Now let's get you dressed for outside. Even if I really like this one-shoulder deal." His thumb caressed my skin before he held up my gray wool coat for me to put on.

I shivered when he flipped my hair out and draped it over my shoulder to make sure it didn't get tangled in my hood. When I glanced back at him, he was so damn close.

Indecision lurked in his eyes. It would be so easy to just let this wicked chemistry lead me upstairs with him in tow. He seemed to understand that as much as we both wanted it, maybe it wasn't a good idea.

Exhaling, he reached for his sweater on the couch and shrugged it on. He should have looked stodgy. Instead, he was all broad shoulders and sinful muscles. A thin leather bracelet peeked from his cuffs. It consisted of a heavy silver bead with some sort of intricate knots that clung to his wide wrist. He was far too intriguing in too many ways.

He pulled on his coat and handed me my red scarf. "Shall we?" He crooked his arm.

I couldn't stop the smile as I slid my arm through his. "We shall."

Even walking through the door made me feel like there was a change in the air. Evening had descended on the town. Just the barest hint of setting sun peeked from the trees over the water. The café was kitty corner from the park. The street lamps had been capped with lanterns to give the street an old world feel.

The gazebo—and scene of the crime—was lit up with white twinkle lights and fat retro bulbs in traditional colors, never mind the glistening tree itself. It reminded me of when I was really young, before my mother forgot what holidays were. When we tried to eke out an existence in the shabby apartment in a small town that was more famous for the waterfall and old factories than anyone who lived there.

My mother had actually made an effort to give me a good Christmas that year. She'd been clear-eyed and not focused on some jerk to take care of her for once. She'd found decorations in the shed behind the old two-family house. We'd strung the ancient lights on the tiny Charlie Brown tree, and we had draped the remaining strings over the window ledge in my bedroom.

The lights on the gazebo shimmered in my vision, and the slap of cold singed my lungs.

Suddenly, I was twirling, and the lights seemed merry rather than sad. Callum caught my hand on the twirl out, and then I was overwhelmed with his cedar scent carrying on the cold breeze. A flashback to yesterday. No snow this time, but just like last night, he was nearly irresistible.

"I don't like that faraway look."

His lips were so close that each word was a small puff of air against mine. Part of me wanted to blurt out the sadness that sneaked up on me this time of year, but the rest…

I didn't want to be the woman with the absentee parents. I was a strong, single woman who was just starting her career.

And I'd be strong and brave right now too.

I leaned in and closed the gap. His tongue was warm and a little too talented, but that was exactly what I needed.

A man who knew what he was doing. If I was going to act a little crazy, then it should be with a guy who knew what the hell he was doing.

The sound of a clearing throat had us pulling apart. Callum dragged his thumb over his lower lip right before he stepped away.

"Sorry to interrupt." The jangle of keys dragged my attention away from the best kisser in the known universe. Well, at least my universe. Goodness.

Dare Kramer held up the keys. He had on a heavy tan jacket and an obviously homemade hat. There was no way he picked that blue out for himself. "We have the order in for the customization we talked about, but for now, we've got you all fixed up."

"Fixed up?"

Callum flushed. "A guy in a truck backed out without looking, and I slid into a ditch."

"Oh. Wow, so that's why you've been hanging out." Disappointment hit me harder than it should have. Of course he'd have a reason besides trying to get me to go out with him.

He took the keys from Dare. "Thanks, man. Do I need to sign anything?"

"Nah. We're all set. I put the receipt in the glove box for your records or if you want to submit it to your insurance."

"Thanks, but my premiums are enough."

Dare chuckled. "I bet. It's a sweet ride. We're excited to work on it. We'll give you a call in a few weeks."

"Sounds good." Callum pocketed his keys then tucked my arm through his. "Heading to the festival?"

"Kelsey dragged me over there earlier for the kid stuff." Dare palmed the top of his head and settled his hat farther back. "My wife."

"Sorry I missed them," I said. "Sean sure is cute in his snowsuit."

"The kid is Houdini. He's always squirming out of it somehow." He shrugged. "I've got tow truck duty, and some asshat already needs my help."

"This asshat appreciates that you guys are so quick." Callum grinned.

"Not touching that one." Dare looked between us. "See you after the New Year."

"Pretty sure that's the most I've ever heard Dare say," I said after Dare ambled off. "He must like you."

"He likes my car."

"That's probably the truth."

"Now where were we?"

"You were distracting me. Across the street, sir."

He inclined his head. "As you wish."

I dragged him across Main Street. "Don't quote *Princess Bride* at me."

"That's it. You're marrying me for real."

A giggle escaped before I could squash it. "We'll see."

We wandered around the vendors who were hawking their wares, and we made sure to have cider and donuts from the nearby Happy Acres orchard. They had quite the entertainment lineup.

When I heard female giggling, I craned my neck. "Look at that crowd."

Callum boosted me up and I grabbed hold of his shoulders. He grinned up at me. "What's happening, do you think? Is it someone famous or one of the three-hundred babies who have overtaken this town?"

I laughed. "A bit of both actually." There was a carriage there for sure, but the long dark hair of a tall man holding court told me it was a bit more. There had been a lot of excitement in Crescent Cove, thanks to my friend Ivy's semi-famous rock producer husband.

He had quite a few famous friends, including one who spent part of the year at Happy Acres.

"Pretty sure that's Ian Kagan over there." I slid down Callum's body. His hands firmed around my waist as he set me on the ground. My nipples tingled through a few layers. What was it about this guy?

He frowned. "Why is that name familiar?"

"Depends on if you listen to the rock stations." I rested my palms on his chest.

"Do you?"

I shrugged. "I enjoy music. We fight over which channel to put it on at the salon."

"Is that right?" He toyed with the ends of my hair. "That's how you did the Cinderella transformation in less than an hour?"

"A woman never tells her secrets." I looked away. Better to remember that I'd be turning back into that pumpkin at midnight.

He nudged my face back toward him. "Lest you forget, it was you who caught my attention yesterday. The girl with messy braids. I'm pretty sure they were pink too."

I blushed. "Yeah, I drew the short straw for testing out a new temporary rinse. Took me four washes to get the cotton candy color out of my hair."

"I enjoyed the pink, but I like the real you."

"How do you know which is the real me? I could change my hair daily."

His lips tipped up. "I'd like to find out."

I stepped back and headed for the gazebo, but he caught up to me at the large oak tree and stopped me with a hand on my arm. "Is that so hard to believe?" he asked.

"What? That you want to get to know me?"

He nodded.

"Yes, actually. You've got the keys to your shiny ride. What's keeping you here?"

"You. Ever since I joined you under that mistletoe."

"Why?"

"Why not?"

I shook my head. "I'm not the girl who—"

"Has fun?"

I blinked. There wasn't an easy answer for that. I worked. I saved. I focused on the future. On finally doing something I loved and was good at. That was my idea of fun. Being stable for the first time in my life. I never wanted for money because I'd learned to budget from a very young age—because I 'd had to or I went hungry.

Fun wasn't part of my life.

"Take a chance on me. With an open mind and—"

"Legs?"

"Why Miss Lawton, that's positively scandalous."

I frowned. "How do you know my last name?"

"The very helpful Mrs. Gunderson. She gave me the skinny on most of the town. I didn't know about the famous rockstar though."

"He doesn't live here. His best friend does, so we see him from time to time."

"Such a peculiar little town."

"You don't know the half of it."

He took my hand again. "Your hands are ice." He took my other one and sandwiched it between both of his. He brought them up to his mouth and blew into the cup he'd made around them. "Pretty sure it's not the only thing thing that's icy."

I stiffened.

"Don't get your back up. Just give me a chance. You've already made up your mind about what we are. And if that's really how you feel, I'll walk away. I'll hate it, and I'll always wonder what if, but I'll respect your wishes, Ellie. Always."

SEVEN

IN THE DISTANCE, A CHEERY BIT OF BELLS AND DRUMS HAD A SMALL CROWD singing along. I braced for the brush off as a guy doing a fair impression of Michael Bublé sang "Please Come Home For Christmas".

Ellie had been looking for reasons to kill our date since we'd been interrupted by Dare. Hell, she'd been looking for a way out before then too, but at least then I'd had a chance. Now she was just searching for a reason to give me the boot.

Couldn't she feel what was between us? Was it all on my side? I'd been attracted to plenty of women over the years. Some I acted on, some didn't live up to the initial spark, and still others were lost opportunities.

I really didn't want this to be the latter.

I curled my larger fingers around hers, but I didn't grip tight. If she wanted to slip away, I'd deal with it. Probably with some pretty strong whisky—the Scottish kind. I was like my father in that regard. Sometimes all you could do was let a smooth Doublewood take care of your problems. As long as it only lasted a day or so.

Maybe a week for this woman.

Even after just a day with her in my bloodstream, it seemed like she would take a fair bit of time to forget—if ever.

She lifted her chin. "Dance with me?"

I hadn't been prepared for that one.

"Or don't you do that sort of thing?" she asked when I didn't reply.

"My mother made sure I could hold my own."

Her eyebrow quirked. "Is that right?"

"Don't get weird. I'm not that much of a mama's boy. But we are a well-rounded bunch."

"Then I guess you need to put your dancing shoes where your mouth is."

"I thought I'd put my foot in my mouth enough since I met you."

Her eyes sparkled in the twinkle lights glowing off the tree above us. "You didn't even try to let me off the hook there."

Her secret little smile was the only answer she gave me.

I drew her through the crowd to the small dance floor to the side of the stage. A jazzy version of Elvis's "Blue Christmas" allowed me to draw her close and slowly sway with her. The music was too loud to talk, but I was happy enough to just enjoy her honey and vanilla scent. I pressed my cheek along her hair as we slowly circled in and around the other couples.

The guy on the stage lengthened the short classic tune with a few bits of flair. And he had a dramatic enough end to the song to let me dip her.

She gave a startled laugh and gripped my arms. I grinned down at her and slowly drew her back up. The song slid into a more upbeat song. Enough that I could do the two-step with her and twirl her between a few different couples.

I had the five pairs surrounding us laughing as we passed around one another. I even ended up dancing with a strapping man who reminded me of Santa for the last quarter of the song before finally ending up with Ellie back in my arms.

Her cheeks were flushed, and she was smiling so wide her cheeks must hurt. And God, she was fucking gorgeous.

The band started another jazzy version of a Christmas standard. She nodded to the edge of the dance floor and made a gesture for a drink.

"I didn't think I could keep up with you. When you said you knew how to dance, you weren't kidding."

I maneuvered her through the small crush of people watching the dancers and we headed for the cider stand. The rockstar had made himself scarce so the line was much shorter now.

"Mom used to love to do the big Christmas shindig," I said as we took our spots at the end of the line. "We've slowed things down over the years, but when my dad was still working at the college, she'd have all the teachers out to the farm. Did it up like it was a prom crossed with a winter dance from the sixties. Now she puts up all the decorations without the crowds."

"That sounds…wow."

"Yeah, my mom doesn't do anything small."

"And your dad is a teacher?"

"Was. He's retired. Writing a book, I think. He's been working on it for a while." I laughed. "Mom keeps him busy."

"Sounds like she's a force."

"Accurate."

We finally got to the front of the line. A stunning woman with darkly-lashed gold eyes smiled at us, but her expression warmed considerably when she recognized my date. "Hey, Ellie."

She waved. "It's been a long time, Zoe. And you're definitely way smaller than the last time I saw you."

"Elvis and my idiot keep me running."

My eyebrows shot up. "Elvis?"

She flipped a massive braid over her shoulder, the color almost as pure as the snow lining the streets. "Don't go there. I blame my fiancé for the name. I was delirious from giving birth, and he took advantage of me."

Ellie absently stepped closer to me as people flowed around us. The band was taking a break, and everyone was looking for refreshments. I curled my arm around her back. She didn't shy away, so I counted that as a win.

Ellie's hand brushed my belt. "I caught Ian holding court."

Zoe rolled her eyes. "I tried to convince him to stay home, but I think he likes seeing people act stupid over him. He's walking the baby around now. Motion usually knocks him out."

"Stick me in the car when I'm not driving, and I'm out like a light." Ellie glanced up at me. "Leaded or unleaded?"

I turned to Zoe. "There's an option?"

She waggled her eyebrows. "My brothers are into the cider and beer deal now too. We have some of those on tap as well."

"Think I'm frozen enough to go for some warm unleaded."

That was evidently the right answer. Ellie nodded. "Same."

"Coming up."

The line prevented more chitchat, and the two women waved goodbye. I glanced around for somewhere to sit. "Why don't we go by the water? I haven't been able to get down to see the big Christmas tree at the end of the pier. I started that way earlier, but the crowds were too thick."

"It's chilly out there."

"Now we've got warm cider, right?"

"Anything you want."

She scraped her teeth over her lower lip before we crossed the lawn to head toward the pier. We were quiet as we sipped from our drinks. The sharp apple with a cinnamon finish was probably the best cider I'd had in a damn long time. I'd finished more than half of mine by the time we stepped onto the pier.

The breeze off the water was brisk, but not nearly as icy as I'd been expecting.

She drew in a lungful of air. "Snow soon."

I grinned down at her. "You can smell snow?"

"Not hard in a lake town. It's nearly every day. But a bit of warmth is always followed by snowflakes."

Cool LED white lights lined the railings of the long pier to the spectacular tree at the end. It was decked out in the fat, vintage Christmas lights like the gazebo. Huge gold and silver stars were tucked in the branches and were probably wired in there to combat the pull of the wind off the water.

But from here, it was like walking into an old postcard, and I appreciated the nostalgia and tradition. So many trees were glammed up and pink these days that it was nice to see something reminiscent of a classic Christmas.

The closer we got to the tree, the softer her face became. "I didn't get to do the tree thing very often as a kid."

I wasn't sure if I should ask for details, but the fact that she'd volunteered something about herself made me wary about screwing up. "Not into holidays?" Though that didn't seem right based on her pure happiness over the decorations and festivities.

"I learned not to be." She leaned on the railing next to the tree and stared across the water. "When I was a teenager, I used to look across the lake and wonder what it was like to be in one of those houses." She pointed to a large home lit up as if it embodied Christmas. "Like the Hamilton house out there. Every holiday, it looked like a postcard. And then in the summer, it was always bustling with posh parties."

"Do you want posh parties?"

She glanced up at me. "Not really my thing. But that house over there..." She pointed to the other side of the lake then braced her arm on the railing and propped her chin on her hand. "That house is more me. Those turrets and skinny windows mixed with grand ones. It's got those gingerbread details and a wraparound porch."

I followed where she pointed. It was decked out for Christmas, but instead of the pristine white lights like the Hamilton house she'd pointed out first, it had huge bulbs I could see from where we were. They lined the roofline, accentuating the sharp angles of the Victorian-style home. "Not usually the kind of house you see on a lake."

"No. It's such an odd little place in the middle of all the traditional Cape Cod styles and super ultra rich people with their modern mansions. And of course the condos that have infiltrated the Cove lately."

"I have a condo."

She wrinkled her nose at me. "Anyway, that's the house I always look at when I let myself dream."

Let herself? I had a feeling that didn't happen all too often. I slid my hand down her back. "Pretty good dream, if you ask me."

She straightened up. "Dreams are just that." She moved toward me fully for the first time since I'd met her. Well, beyond our first kiss. She'd melted into me under the mistletoe like taffy on a ninety-degree day, but I'd been chasing her ever since.

While I appreciated the chase, I wondered how it would end.

"How are you with fantasies?"

I swallowed. "Not that I'm complaining—because believe me, I'm not—but this is a bit of a change in mood."

The glow from the tree lit half her face. Her smile was slow and a little dangerous. "I've been convincing myself all night not to let myself enjoy you. I'm sure you'll be taking that hot little car out of town by morning."

"How do you know it's a hot little car?"

"Dare's eyes lit up like it was a dream. Pretty sure it's either a muscle car or one with an engine that men lust after."

I shrugged and dragged in a quick breath when her fingers slid under my coat then along my sweater. I cleared my throat. "Engine."

Her touch wandered lower. Her head was still tipped enough that she looked at me through her lashes. "Are you compensating?"

"Would I own up to it if I was?"

"Hmm. That's true. Most men can't gauge size."

Not one to be outmaneuvered, I inched my hand into her coat and coasted over her hip to her spectacular ass.

Her breath hitched this time. The sound turned into a long exhale as I pulled her tight against me to show her just how adequate I was. Her nails dug into my plaid shirt, and I took a damn chance.

I'd been gambling on her all day. I wasn't going to stop now.

She was right—we didn't have a lot of time. Christmas was almost here, and I was tempted to invite her back to my folks' house. But I had a feeling that would make her jackrabbit faster than the White Rabbit. Only her important date didn't include me.

And I really wanted to change her mind.

I lowered my mouth to hers. Instead of pressing in on her with the need so readily flourishing between us, I took it easy. I gentled my explorations with a slow, drugging kiss. Cinnamon and apples mixed with her unique flavor, and I would've willingly drowned in her forever.

Her hands slid up to grip my shoulders. I cupped her face and tilted her head back to deepen the kiss. The crowd had thinned, and we were practically alone out here with only the lapping water and the deep night cloaked around us. We were far enough from the festival that it was only her quickened breath playing as our soundtrack.

A sound I'd be glad to hear much more of.

"Come to my room with me," I said against her mouth. "We both need that fantasy."

I'd been so wrapped up in my classes and stressing about a new project for my agent that there'd been little time for me to tend to my own needs.

Seeing her, tasting her, and wanting her had brought them back into such crisp focus, I literally ached. And maybe after one night, I could convince her for more. I had a feeling that once wouldn't be nearly enough for either of us.

"A fantasy," she said with a nod. "Yes."

I brought my other hand up to cup her cool cheek. "I'm at The Hummingbird's Nest."

"Guess we need to go get your car. It's a bit of walk, and I'm freaking cold."

I laughed. "Then let's get you warmed up."

"I'm sure you have a few ideas for that."

"You know what they say…"

"Skin on skin is the quickest way to warm up?"

"Damn, I like the way you think."

EIGHT

Ellie

THE HEATER WAS BLASTING IN CALLUM'S INSANELY BRIGHT CAR. EVEN IN the dark of Dare's parking garage, it was like a neon banana. However, when the engine purred, I couldn't deny I enjoyed that bit of extra testosterone.

It was already thick in the air anyway. He'd practically dragged me over to the garage. Not that I could blame him. I'd been wishy washy in the extreme. Talk about hot and cold—even in my own mind.

Now that I'd given him the green light, he was going to run with it.

I wasn't used to being impulsive. That was my mother. And watching her make the same mistakes over and over again with men made me so careful not to do the same.

I glanced over at him in the shadows of the car. The bright blue lights of the various dials and speedometer tossed his face into stark relief. The hollowed out cheekbones and square jawline gave him that classically handsome look that made women stupid.

Clearly, I wasn't immune.

He curled his fingers around the shifter, and then he paused and directed all that ridiculous beauty my way. "This doesn't have to go any further than our date night. I can drop you home and pick you up and take you out for a proper dinner tomorrow."

I stuffed down the urge to laugh. "A proper dinner on Christmas Eve?"

He shrugged. "Or I can cook you dinner."

"Is that right? At The Hummingbird's Nest?"

"No, my place. Well-rounded, remember?"

I leaned into him, and he met me halfway. "Just take me to your room." I said it against his mouth, the demand oddly reminiscent of how he'd been trying to convince me to go out with him all day.

He cupped the back of my head and kissed me hard before sitting straight again and fastening his seatbelt. I did the same and stared out the window at all the lights swaying in the increasing wind off the water.

There was a lot of pedestrian traffic, so our trip was slow going. We were a hearty bunch in the Cove, but most of the vendors were starting to pack it in. People had families to get to and holiday plans to finalize. And here I was with a stranger, feeling more at home with him than I did with most of my friends.

Not sure what that said about me—or maybe him.

He was so easy with everyone he met. I was polite and friendly, but not like him. He just instantly took to people. And to be truthful, they took to him. Dancing in the park like he'd choreographed it himself. Not missing a beat even when Mr. Phillips ended up in his arms. He was our town Santa and that dance had been the sweetest thing I'd ever seen.

And the sexiest.

Callum was so at ease within his own skin that he was able to be sweet, sexy, or funny in an instant.

I wanted to see all the other sides of him.

He gave me an absent smile as he turned up the radio. An old Creed song was on, and he exaggeratedly sang "Arms Wide Open" until I was laughing with him instead of overthinking everything.

The ride to The Hummingbird's Nest was over before it started. He pulled into the winding road, and we sang along to the next song as he parked. An old Keith Urban song went through a few stages—from messing up lyrics, to laughing, to kissing.

I couldn't get enough of his mouth. It was full and warm and oh so talented. He nipped at my lower lip until I practically climbed into his lap to get closer.

He opened his door, and the slap of cold air broke us apart. He quickly got out and came around to help me out of of the low slung car with more kisses and laughter.

"You're so damn beautiful." He threaded his fingers through my hair. "Unbelievably beautiful."

I flushed and looked down. "You've got me here. You don't have to pour it on." I leaned back into his car to get my bag from the floor.

"Evidently, I do." He circled my waist and hauled me against him. "It's not just physical, Ellie. I keep catching these flashes of something under that serious face. When you let yourself enjoy the moment, you glow."

"Stop."

"I'm an artist. Do you know how hard I look for that glow? And it's in the most random of people. A woman in her nineties I found at a park. She was feeding pigeons of all things. Greta Bloom. I'll never forget her. She had that light. And here you are with the same one, but you also have so much more."

He lowered his mouth to mine and I gave in. I didn't even care if it was a line at this point. He made me feel like there was something warm and bright inside of me, and I was willing to believe to keep this feeling.

We stumbled our way up to the entrance, barely able to keep our hands off one another. There was a crush of people at the main desk, probably overflow from the festival. Because he was already settled in a room, we were able to sneak around and head for the stairs.

I wasn't paying attention and nearly wiped out on the small caution sign.

"Shit." He lifted me and hauled me over one of the signs that explained they were renovating.

The stairs were an old spiral style, and we kept bouncing off the railing and one another as we tripped our way upstairs and down the hallway to his room. He fumbled with his key and backed into the room, dragging me in with him. Coats hit the floor, and his sweater followed them before he went to work on his shirt buttons.

I flipped my own sweater over my head, and he stopped in the middle of the room. "Sweet Zeus."

I frowned. That seemed like an odd phrase, but I didn't have time to think about it. I needed to help him out of his shirt. There were far too many buttons. We both fumbled with the tiny pearlescent disks. My fingers shook and his were too large.

My goodness, he was proportional. Finally, we got them all, and I pushed the gold and gray plaid shirt off his shoulders. Before I could get it down his wrists, they were caught. We'd forgotten the buttons at his cuffs.

He was at my mercy and I kinda liked it.

He kept trying to get his wrists free as I scraped my nails through the just-right amount of hair on his chest. It covered his extremely impressive pecs and arrowed down his lean torso with a lighter and silkier texture. I brushed my cheek along the softness and kissed my way down his abs.

"Ellie."

My name was a strangled moan as I dropped to my knees. I flicked my tongue over the little divot of his navel. "It's been a little while since I've done this, but I think I remember how this goes." I jerked the tail of his belt free from the loops and loosened his buckle.

His cock curved up against his zipper, bulging for freedom. I flicked open the button of his jeans and slowly peeled down his zipper. The chili pepper boxers I revealed made me laugh.

"Better be the boxers you're laughing at, woman." He finally got his hands free from the shirt and tried to draw me up to my feet.

I shook my head then reached in for my prize. His stormy eyes went heavy and dark as I dragged the flat of my tongue along the underside of his length. A hint of that cedar scent hit me just before the salty, earthy flavor of him made my mouth water. I took more of him, swallowing down his taste and wanting more.

His head dropped back and his throat worked as he groaned my name. Spurred on by it, I took him again and again, coating him enough for me to palm his length and suck harder until he finally raked his fingers through my hair to stop me.

"God, that feels so good. I don't want to come in your mouth first. I want you wrapped around me. Under me—fuck, even over me. Just not like this."

I drew him deeper until the velvety head of his cock hit the back of my throat. I wanted to make him come. I could taste the power of it. As if he was a conduit to something bigger and more important. A freedom I'd been searching for all of my life.

Taking something for myself.

Taking *him* for myself.

He bent over to me and freed himself with a hiss. "I've never wanted a woman so badly. Please."

I wiped my mouth, but he shook his head and lifted me, kissing me with wild abandon. Dirty and deep until I could scarcely breathe around it. I wrapped my legs around his waist, and he turned enough to get us onto the bed.

I wiggled higher, and he dragged at the cups of my strapless bra. "I wondered if you had one of these female contraptions under that sweater." His eyes were almost black as he inched it down my ribs then yanked it around to get to the hooks. "Off. Off." I tried to shimmy higher on the mattress, but he was having none of that. He bore down on me as he tossed the scrap of satin over his shoulder. "There you are." He tugged on one nipple and dragged his beardy chin over the other before licking it lightly. "My turn."

"Turn?" I arched up off the bed as he twisted my nipple to just the edge of pain. The blood bloomed like fire under my skin, and warmth pooled in my belly. Pooled lower as I moved my hips restlessly. His cock was right there trapped between us.

He pressed it along my thigh as he shifted lower to get the button of my jeans undone. Again, he dragged his chin over my skin. Goosebumps rose and covered me from neck to toes. "Callum."

"Say it again." He traced the tip of his tongue along the lace edge of my panties, just under my bellybutton.

"Callum."

He smiled against the light pink lace. "I'll hear that in my dreams."

I closed my eyes. I didn't want to think about him dreaming of me. I only wanted to think of the now—the pleasure from this ill-advised plan. Not the nebulous future I couldn't control.

Then he tucked his tongue under the elastic and groaned at what he found there. Nothing but skin and me. "Ellie."

He peeled my jeans and panties down and growled. Wasn't sure I'd ever heard a guy growl about me. He fumbled with my stretchy boots and finally got them off. He shoved his shoulders between my thighs and opened me wide then dragged his chin over my flesh to the absolutely bare skin around my slit.

Working at a salon meant I had access to all sorts of personal grooming. And keeping our Brazilian techniques sharp in a small town meant sometimes we had to practice on each other.

"Beautiful." He glanced up at me as he traced his tongue along my swollen center.

I lifted my hips to either help him along or push him away. I wasn't sure which. It was too much and too invasive for a first time. And yet hadn't I done the same? Here was my tit for tat. I was pretty sure I wouldn't be pushing him away in the final moment as he'd done to me.

Reaching up toward the headboard, I only found pillows. I couldn't breathe around the rasping play of his tongue along every nerve ending inside me. When I couldn't move away from the onslaught of his lips and then the pressure of his finger sliding inward, I gave up and cupped my breast to tug at my nipple.

I was on the edge and crazed with it. No self-induced orgasms were like this. They were perfunctory when my insomnia got too bad, and it was the only way to knock my ass out. This was all-consuming as he watched me flail.

His nostrils flared as he held onto me and spread me wider. I tried to buck him off me, afraid the entire floor would hear my sounds. Finally, I grabbed one of the pillows behind me and screamed into it. The broken sobs had me curling into myself, but he wouldn't allow it.

He wanted inside every part of me.

Quickly, he climbed up and took the pillow from me, replacing it with his mouth. The wildness of my own taste was a chain reaction. He slid two fingers inside me and rode out the scream. I tasted blood as our teeth clashed in the shuddering chatter of my overwhelmed system.

He was right there with me. He swore and scraped his teeth down my neck as I cried out his name over and over. There was no generic cry for God. There was only Callum and the maelstrom of pleasure. When he fumbled between us, I recognized the unmistakable feel of latex, and then it just didn't matter. He was filling me, driving into me and chasing the end of my orgasm and demanding more. And I gave it. I gave him everything without thought to the aftermath.

I wrapped myself around him and accepted all of him. The sweat and the hardness, the power and the insanity. It shouldn't be this good. It shouldn't feel like everything.

But it was.

It did.

"Ellie. Come with me." He slid one hand between us and the friction and the fullness were no match for self-preservation. I dug my nails into his back as he thrust into me again and again. And the one orgasm clawed into two.

He pinned me to the mattress and groaned against my neck then found my mouth as we held on to one another. I didn't realize there were tears until he kissed them away and slowly, the room came back into focus.

The muscles I hadn't used in well over a year shrieked even as I wanted to roll over and sleep for a lifetime. "Glorious," I murmured into his skin.

He laughed and lightly kissed my shoulder. "You may not say the same when you see what I did to your neck." He drew his thumb over an abrasion before he rolled off me with a wince.

We lay side by side, our breathing still labored. Eventually, he rolled off the bed and disappeared into the bathroom. The sound of water running and the flush of a toilet roused me from the near coma I'd slipped into.

He shifted me under the covers and kissed me. "I'm freaking famished."

I cuddled into the cool white pillow and could have happily drifted off. "I should go."

"No, stay. I'm going to go get us something to eat."

I needed to go. Ties came with each minute I lingered in the afterglow. But the bed was so warm, and everything was so soft.

Including me.

He pressed a kiss to my forehead. "I'll be right back."

"'Kay," I mumbled.

I should really go.

NINE

I RESISTED THE URGE TO WHISTLE MY WAY DOWN THE STAIRS. ENDING UP in Crescent Cove had been a lucky break after all.

Now if I could just figure out how to keep Ellie in my life for more than a few more mind-blowing hours...

One thing at a time.

First, I would make sure the rest of the evening went as well as it had started.

I headed downstairs as soundlessly as possible. A few of the steps creaked, so I made sure not to make too much noise.

I wasn't trying to hide exactly. I just didn't want to be noticed.

Or questioned.

Or gossiped about.

The elegantly appointed foyer beckoned. Sconces high on the wall flickered as if lit by candles. Tasteful Christmas bells and garland dripped from the reservations counter, and cheerful holiday carols played from recessed speakers. The air was scented with cinnamon and nutmeg. All seemed perfectly welcoming.

Yet once I reached the bottom stair, I didn't move.

It wasn't terribly late, but the desk seemed deserted. That was good news for me. I'd grab some sodas and salty snacks from the vending machines off the foyer, and hopefully, a few condoms. Even a dignified establishment such as this should be prepared with typical vacation items, right?

Razors, pretzels, and rubbers. Seemed like a usual bed and breakfast shopping list.

I found the sodas. The salty treats. The sweet ones. And a discreet sign that said, "For personal care items, consult the desk."

Inwardly, I groaned. Probably outwardly too.

We'd already had sex. Amazing, life-changing, jingle my balls off sex. I wanted more of it. I was pretty sure she did too. There were plenty of other ways to enjoy ourselves without the need for protection, but I couldn't deny getting back into the sweet clasp of Ellie's body was at the top of tonight's agenda.

So, I was just going to go to the desk. They probably had other people manning it during the off-hours anyway. Sage Hamilton couldn't be there all night long.

"Hi, there," Sage said cheerfully when I rang the bell for service. She'd popped up from behind the counter.

I managed not to stumble backward but only narrowly. Did she hide behind there to surprise all the guests or was I just special?

"Hi, Sage. Late for you, isn't it?"

"Oh, it's almost Christmas, so we gave Alyce the night off. She's usually the one who handles the desk after hours."

"That must be hard on you."

"Not so much, no. We'll close early tomorrow, and Oliver—my husband—is watching our daughter. It gives me a night off, to tell you the truth."

"But you're working...?" I regretted asking as soon as the half-formed question was out.

"It gives me a night off from babymaking practice."

"Oh. Um. Okay. Good luck with that."

"We just kicked into high gear for our second kid, and the man is relentless. Give him a target, and he insists on shooting his gun over and over. But it's fun for the most part. Just requires lots of stamina and hydration. Have you tried those vitamin waters? We have some in the vending machine. I recommend them for long sessions, if you know what I mean." She waggled her brows, and I was fairly certain my kneecaps blushed.

But it also gave me a nice segue into what I needed. I would even extend this painful conversation if it led to more condoms. Preferably a few.

"That's why I'm here actually."

"Oh, I guessed. You had that look. Plus, all of that stuff." She gestured to the items in my arms. "You have the munchies. Been there, done that."

"Right." I might die right in this very spot.

"It's a different kind of munchies than you get after taking marijuana. At least I assume. I haven't tried that myself." She frowned. "You're not smoking in the room, are you? That's prohibited in Section IV of the agreement you signed."

"No, of course not. I wouldn't do that here."

Or anywhere, at least not since college. If I stayed down here much longer, she'd probably know all about my days at the university too.

"I should hope not. How many do you need?"

Now the flush was steadily moving up my body. Soon, my nose would be redder than Rudolph's. "Do you have a…package?"

"Yes. Three, six, and fifteen."

"Wow, that's quite a jump."

"You always save when you buy in bulk." Her cherubic face was so serious I wasn't sure if she was kidding until she grinned. "It's almost Christmas. Consider this my gift to you. Be sure to put a nice note in the guest book. Don't mention the freebies though. I don't want to shake loose the bargain hunters." She slid an organza-covered box tied with a bow my way.

I laughed so hard that one of our snacks went flying.

After I collected it, I tucked the box of condoms next to the pretzels in my arms. "Well, thanks. You're all heart, Sage."

She beamed. "I am, that's why I'm going to warn you—you probably don't need those. Unless you've had a vasectomy? And you look too young for that." She waved a hand while I stared and wondered if we'd launched into another dimension. "Sorry, I'm getting too personal. Bad habit of mine. I just consider all of my guests to be staying in my home, so we're more than friends, we're family. Anyway, merry ho-ho-ho."

"No, I haven't had a vasectomy. What do you mean? Don't need them, why?"

"You haven't heard about Crescent Cove?"

Why, yes, now that she'd mentioned it, I'd heard about unplanned pregnancies related to the Cove. But that had to be like an old wives' tale or something.

Even if it wasn't, too late now. Still, the odds were in my favor.

Probably.

"Heard what?" I asked.

She bit her lip, her blue eyes getting even wider. "Let's just say we're having a baby boom. A lot of women come to town and end up getting pregnant. Quickly. Our tourism is up thirty-eight percent this year just due to that bit of legend and lore."

The logical side of my brain immediately threw up a roadblock. "If that's so, why are you needing to practice so much?"

"Oh, I could be pregnant already. We just enjoy the process." She laughed. "Happy holidays!"

I went back upstairs in a zombie-like state. I couldn't even claim not to believe what Sage had just claimed—that a propensity towards pregnancy might as well be in the water—since I was a mythology professor. Fantastical tales were my lifeblood.

Had I somehow stepped into one?

I unlocked the door to find Ellie sitting in the middle of my bed, her hair a riot of waves around her bare shoulders. She pulled the sheet up to cover herself, and her eyes were soft from sleep. "What time is it?"

"Just a bit after ten."

"Oh." She swung her legs over the side. "I should really head home."

I crossed to her, dumping my bounty on the bed. "I got us some snacks and drinks."

The ribbon-wrapped care package landed beside her leg. She picked it up. "A present?"

"Sort of a present for us both."

She tucked a lock of hair behind her ear then turned over the box.

The rattle inside made her laugh. "Presents for us, indeed." She loosened the bow and laughed again. "Ribbed for her pleasure, at least."

"Bonus points to Sage."

"Do I want to know?"

I grinned. "Uh, probably not."

The echo of Sage's warning about the baby boom in town should have tempered my lust, but it seemed to only get me more excited to break into the box.

After a Snickers bar.

I grabbed the candy bar and broke it in half then offered her the still-wrapped portion.

She took it, trading it for the box of condoms.

I set the box on the bedside table before sitting beside her. "Stay tonight."

She looked down at her candy and fiddled with the wrapper. "I really shouldn't."

"We've already taken the plunge. No going back now."

The corner of her mouth tipped up. "That's true." She took a bite of the candy and peeked around me. "Are those potato chips?"

"Why, yes, they are."

"Gimme."

I grinned and handed them over. "So, that means I can have the Doritos?"

"Maybe. Only if you brush your teeth."

I leaned in and nipped a kiss before she could pop a chip in her mouth. "Deal."

I stood and went to my new suitcase and pulled out a vintage concert T-shirt for her. She took it gratefully and pulled it on.

I picked up three different bottles of soda. "I wasn't sure of your— okay, Dr. Pepper it is."

She cracked the seal. "I pretty much drink coffee or Diet Coke but since it's here." She took a long swallow and sighed. "My mom loved this stuff. I used to scrape together tip money for her twelve-pack cans. Sometimes I'd sneak a can for myself."

Scraped?

I had so many questions. Little slips from her about a less than stellar childhood made me ache for her. My household growing up had been noisy and full of laughter. A lot of fighting too. Far too many boys in one house meant a lot of strife in between pranks and enough laundry to ensure my mom taught me to be self-sufficient from an early age.

But being self-sufficient was a big difference from what she was talking about.

She popped another chip in her mouth with a sigh. "Didn't realize I was so hungry."

"We sort of skipped dinner."

She peered into the snack-sized bag. "Not a big deal."

Now I felt like an asshole. I hadn't even fed her, for God's sake. We'd been wrapped up in each other and caught up in the push and pull of attraction. Food definitely hadn't been at the top of my menu. "Is that diner near the park an all-night kind of deal?"

"Normally, but with the festival, not so much."

"Ahh."

"Don't worry about feeding me, Callum. I'm more of a small meals and snacks kind of woman. When you work as many jobs as I have, snagging food between shifts is the norm."

"It doesn't have to be that way."

She dug into the bag for the last chip then licked the tips of her fingers. "You're right, but I like my life this way. And working full-time at the salon probably won't change the eating on the run thing."

I leaned in and caught a salty kiss. "Or how about a very thoughtful partner who brings his girl dinner for her breaks?"

She smiled into another kiss. "Sounds pretty nice."

The fact that I could picture that so easily made my chest burn. I rolled her under me on the bed. "I'll make it up to you with a huge breakfast."

She didn't answer me, just welcomed me into her arms with a greedy kiss.

Snacks, dinner, and anything else fell out of my head. Her salty taste made me crave more. I slid my hand up under the T-shirt, coasting my fingertips over her silky flesh. I nipped her chin as my thumb rolled over her tight nipple. They were so damn sensitive. She'd practically crawled out of her skin the moment I touched her.

It only made me want to draw out every damn touch. I'd rushed the first time. Feeling her come apart under my mouth had put me on a one-way collision with impatience. My singular focus had been getting that clasping warmth around me.

I'd almost climbed on her without protection. At the last minute, I'd remembered my wallet and the sole condom in there. And the only reason I had one was because of my brother's sense of humor. Hudson had stuck a trio in my stocking last year. And yeah, a year's worth of sex left me with just one.

Again, every part of this situation so wasn't me.

But I wanted it to be. I wanted to hold onto this feeling for longer than just a night. She was worth more than a few stolen hours. I needed to show her that.

I slowed down each touch until her sighs ended in my name. Her legs shifted under me until she could curl one around my hip, dragging me in closer.

"You're killing me," she said as she bit my earlobe. "Inside me. Use that lovely wrapped present, dammit."

"You want my present?"

She rolled her eyes, but there was laughter dancing in those dark depths. She slipped her hand between us and into my jeans. "If I say yes, will you get the show on the road?"

"Why are you in such a hurry?"

In lieu of an answer, she used some damn impressive muscles to flip me over. She shoved up the thermal shirt I'd been wearing and went for my zipper. "Where's that box?"

I groaned and lifted my hips to help her get a better hold on me. I fumbled for the box next to us, and she plucked it out of my hands. Before I could say her name, she had the foil ripped and was rolling it down my cock.

She climbed on me and slid slowly down my length. I groaned at her perfect heat and could only hold on. Her head fell back, and her nipples were rock hard against the vintage Hysteria shirt I'd purchased the night before. The shirt that I'd never wear without thinking about this moment.

I shifted so I could sit up and get a taste of her. I pushed at the soft cotton and found her even softer skin. I sucked on one taut tip and tugged at the other until she straightened and met my gaze. Her hair was a halo of honey-brown waves, and her teeth were scoring her lower lip.

I thrust up into her, and the sounds she'd been holding back tumbled free with my name wrapped in a sigh. I banded my arms around her back and held her against me, tipping her hips forward to get deeper. I'd climb inside her if I could. "God, you feel good. So wet and warm," I said against her neck. "Like you were made for me."

Her eyes widened just before they closed. I gripped her hair to get her to open them again, but she kept them shut. Almost as if she could block me out.

Hell, I wasn't just the conduit for her damn pleasure.

I flipped us over and lifted her thigh higher around my ribs. Her eyes popped wide, and the strangled scream she let out eased the tension inside me.

I lowered my mouth and kissed her hard, invading every part of her —tongue, cock, heart. It wasn't just fucking. It wasn't just pleasure. I wanted it to be more. Maybe that made me stupid, but it was honest.

As she arched under me, her nails dug into my shoulders, and she tightened around me, her breath fast and labored. She was close, and I wanted to go with her. My knuckles dug into the mattress as I sped up to catch her. To never let her go.

She said my name on a shattered cry, and then it was nothing but *her* name on my lips as I finally emptied myself inside of her.

I fell on top of her, my knees and back giving out. Suddenly, I was boneless.

Possibly paralyzed too.

I pressed my face into her neck, dragging in that honeyed vanilla scent that clung to her. And maybe a little bit of me was mixed with her now.

The thought made me greedy enough to wish I could have her all over again.

Once certain body parts rejuvenated anyway.

I gently pulled out of her, holding the edge of the condom as I rolled off her. Then I sat up and looked over at her. She had her arm over her face, and she was still breathing hard.

Carefully, I nudged her arm away so I could see her. "It's never been like this for me either."

She glanced away.

I tugged back her chin so she would look at me. Her eyes were so damn sad. "Is that so bad?"

She rolled onto her side before tucking her hand under a pillow, but she didn't answer me.

I blew out a breath and went into the bathroom to take care of the condom.

When I came back out, she was waiting for me. I took it as a good sign that she was still wearing my T-shirt instead of changing into her clothes. She touched my chest briefly then slid past me and closed the door behind her.

Dammit, why was everything so hard with her? Couldn't she see how good we were together? Would it really be so awful trying to make this work?

Maybe I *was* an asshole.

Padding over to the bench near the dresser in my room, I pulled out my notebook from my messenger bag and sat down. Now that I knew more about her, I could fill in some of the blurrier details. The little mole beside her chin and another on the edge of her collarbone. The hoops she wore.

I didn't know how long she was in the bathroom, but when I looked up, she was staring down at my drawing.

Her eyebrows knitted as she drank in the details—including the red scarf I'd adjusted on the form. It was an undulating ribbon of cashmere dancing around her curves.

"Are you drawing me?"

"Drew, actually." I turned the pad around so she could get a better look.

"Naked?"

"Well, it was more of a wish fulfillment thing at first. This crazy-beautiful girl kisses me under the mistletoe—"

"And so, you what? Go for an anime version of me with lusher tits and ass?"

"No." I looked down at the drawing. "Okay, so it's a little more of an idealized woman instead of you."

"Thanks."

"No." I growled. "It's coming out wrong. I just drew you because I couldn't get you out of my head. And now you're here, and I wanted to capture you." I set the notebook down and touched the little mole on her chin. "The *real* you."

I traced the back of my knuckles down her neck. "Longer, more elegant neck and finer shoulders. Beautiful, firm breasts." I cupped her for a moment before sliding down to her hips and the scrap of lace she'd put back on.

I dug my fingers into her hips and drew her closer to me. "The real woman I'm getting to know is the one I want, not the moment's fantasy."

She was still frowning, but she didn't pull away. "It's a lot, Callum."

"I'm an artist—for real. It's how I process things. It was the only thing I could do to figure out how to keep the moment."

"But I'm naked."

I huffed out a half laugh. "Well, I'm still a guy. And you're so goddamn beautiful, you stole my brain cells." I lifted my hands to cup her face. "I admit it, I'm a little weird. But you have a notebook full of floating heads from magazines that you attacked with scissors and glue."

She laughed and relaxed a little. "I suppose that's true."

I pressed a light kiss to her mouth and led her back to bed. "Stay with me tonight."

"I should really head home."

I flicked back the covers. "I promise I won't ask for more if you still want to leave in the morning. I hope I can change your mind." I took her hand and toyed with the ring on her thumb. I'd need to add that to the drawing. "Give me tonight, at least."

She sat on the mattress and tucked her legs under the sheet. I turned out the light and slid in beside her. Sometimes the dark was an easier place to talk. I curled her into my body, my front to her back until she relaxed against my chest.

"Tell me about your new job."

She settled into the abundance of pillows. "It's not really new."

"Feels new."

"More like advancing from intern to novice."

"Explain."

"I've been going to night school—or day. However you want to put it. Part time for a really long time. In between working two jobs, I was able to get some experience at the salon while I took all the certification classes. But I also had to get so many hours in at the school salon. It was a lot of hair-cutting for free. Well, mostly free. I was able to get some tips on the side, but the school does cheap haircuts to get people to come in. The one nice thing is I learned to cut all hair types. It broadened my training, going slower."

She lightly drew her nails up and down my arm as she spoke of the various hardships of training to get ready to go out into the real world. Like an apprenticeship. I likened it to my own job. I'd worked as a teaching assistant for peanuts until I'd finally finished my education to be a professor.

I'd felt like something was missing, so I'd turned to art. I understood some of what she was describing.

"Because school took so long, I feel like I can go right to a booth rental at Melody's shop."

I threaded my fingers through her hair as she spoke about her dreams. For the first time, it seemed like I was getting to know her.

At least it was a start.

"I can work for myself, finally. No one else."

"Seems like you've been doing that all along."

"It's different." Her voice was getting drowsy. "I actually think I'm ready for the first time."

I continued to stroke her hair, a sensation of peace coming over me. This was right where I was supposed to be. She was exactly who—and what—I'd been meant to find.

Her deep, even breathing dragged me along into dreams as well. I dreamed of her in a strange old house with rooms of all different sizes. A maze of a place full of towers and large glass arches. Her voice was a soft echo full of laughter, but it always seemed just out of reach.

Finally, I found her on the wraparound porch. A white dress shirt teased her thighs, and those big gold hoop earrings glinted almost as brightly as her smile.

A knock at the door dragged me out of the dream.

Sun slanted into the room. I rolled over, but the sheets had long ago cooled.

She was gone.

I stumbled out of bed and jerked on my jeans. Another knock had me scrubbing my face with my hands to wake up. "What?"

"Maid service."

"Can you come back?"

"Yes, sir."

I glanced around the room. There wasn't a trace of her left. Her coat, her bag, and even her scarf were all gone this time.

Disappointment carved through me, quick and sharp.

I trudged into the bathroom to do my business then brushed my teeth. I didn't want to wash her off my skin quite yet.

I went back into the main part of my room and saw something white propped up on my notebook on the dresser.

You gave me one of the loveliest Christmases that I can remember. I haven't had a whole lot to smile about in the last few years, but you gave me that. I'm sorry I couldn't stay. It's just easier this way.

Thank you, Callum.

ELLIE

I crinkled the note and swore. I thought I'd gotten through to her. Thought she might have given us a chance. I wanted to go after her to try to make her see what she was throwing away.

But I couldn't.

I'd promised her she could walk away if that was what she really wanted.

I tossed the note into the trash bin and headed for the shower.

Evidently, it was time to leave Crescent Cove in my rearview mirror.

TEN

Ellie

Valentine's Day

I PUSHED THE BROOM ACROSS THE CLAY-COLORED MATTE TILE. CLIPPINGS from a half dozen clients shuffled along the floor in front of my favorite rubber broom. It had been a busy morning. People excited for a romantic evening had come in for last-minute beautifications.

My book was slowly growing with customers. Some were from the Cove thanks to my years at Brewed Awakening and before that at Robbie's Pizza.

I'd made plenty of acquaintances in town. Enough that I was able to network a little with help from a few coupons. I'd also been doing some videos on the Instagram and TikTok accounts I'd convinced Melody to try out. I was in charge of them, but I actually didn't mind it. Our followers were slowly increasing due to some clever hashtags as well.

All the books I'd read and workshops I'd taken in marketing over the years were finally proving useful. With a little luck from walk-ins and word of mouth, things seemed to be looking up.

I'd given myself six months of savings in a special slush account to cover living expenses, booth rental, and of course my apartment rent. If I really needed to dip into my nest egg, I could. Budgeting had been my life for a long time. Long enough that I still lived way below my means even though I didn't have to anymore.

I was already seeing steady growth in my bank account, especially since I'd established multiple payment options to accommodate younger clients. Melody, the owner of the salon, was still living with a cash and carry setup for the most part, but I was slowly getting her to come around to my way of thinking.

All in all, I was happy.

But I was always tired. A good kind of tired most of the time. Falling into bed after working a full day doing what I loved was a new feeling. And okay, maybe I was going to bed before nine o'clock most nights. It was winter, and the days were shorter.

February was made for sleeping in when I could, and I'd found a lot of joy in making some improvements in the salon. Melody hadn't exactly been on board right away, but money talked. Clients were already commenting on how spa-like the place felt. I'd also used my own cash and time. I'd become comfortable with do-it-yourself ideas years ago because money hadn't been abundant for most of my life.

In the end, Melody thought we could charge a little more because we looked so posh.

I'd done that. My ideas and my ingenuity. Self-pride was new to me, but it felt good.

Most nights I was too tired to think about the man who'd come into my life like a spring storm. Wild and messy, full of wind and excitement. Just as fast as he'd arrived, I knew he'd be gone.

I'd made sure to leave first.

I wasn't sure I could have handled him walking away. It was humbling to know that. He'd overwhelmed me not only physically, but with the way he saw me. That fantasy drawing he'd done of a seductive, almost playful woman—that wasn't who I was.

At least I didn't think so.

Sooner or later, he'd see that and lose interest. It had happened many times in my life to my mother and I. Hot and heavy passion was easy, but there was rarely any lasting substance.

And Callum was an artist, for God's sake. There was no stability there. No peace. And I couldn't allow myself to wonder or hope. Not now. Not when I was just putting my plans into motion.

I had a stubborn side, one I stuffed under the bed each morning. After the lonely nights that made me wonder a bit too much. That insane little voice that said *what if?* It was the same one who wouldn't let me delete the message from Kinleigh with Callum's phone number.

I hadn't been expecting her call the week between Christmas and New Year's. I hadn't recognized the number, but I knew Kinleigh's sweet voice as she left a rambling explanation about the man who'd been looking for me. And she had a gut feeling that I should give him a chance.

Maybe I thought about him sometimes when the day was slow, or the night was long. Maybe I almost called him once or five times.

Suddenly, the floor wavered in my vision. I leaned to the left, and if I hadn't had the broom handle to hold on to, I would have gone down.

"Whoa, Ellie." Paisley Jones, the third stylist in the salon, rushed over to me. Her freakishly strong fingers gripped my upper arm and pushed me into the chair at her station. "You all right?"

"Yeah, just got a little lightheaded there for a second." Had I eaten today? Nothing appealed lately. "Could you grab my water bottle?"

"Yeah, sure, babe." Paisley rushed over to my area at the back of the salon and returned with my purple bottle. "Here. Drink up. Have you eaten?"

I shrugged while I gulped the cool water.

"Want me to run over to the diner or Jersey's for a sandwich?"

I wrinkled my nose. "Everything tastes so *ugh* lately." I took another deep drag on my straw.

"I wish. I just entered shark week. I could hoover down everything from the diner's menu right now. Especially Gina's new poutine addition. Dear God, that's good."

I huffed out a laugh. We could definitely agree there. "Salt is the primary ingredient in my period week menu."

"Doesn't help the ankles, but gawd, so good." She yanked open her drawer and pulled out her phone. "Now I gotta make an order, dammit. You sure you don't want?"

"No, I…" I hadn't wanted anything salty in a while. Not in the last month at all. "Shit." I slid out of her chair and ran for my station.

"Hey, don't move so fast. I don't want to scrape you out of the hair, girl."

"Right. Crap." I turned around to finish my chore.

Paisley waved me off then grabbed the broom. "I got it."

"Thanks."

She already had her cell at her ear and was chitchatting with someone at the diner.

I quickly went for my own drawer and phone. "I'm running to the bathroom, Melody!" I called out.

"Okay!"

"No, no. Don't do this to me." I shut myself into our small water closet and opened my period tracker app.

Six days late.

"Oh, shit." I collapsed onto the little bench full of more plants. I shoved them over to make room for my butt.

I tipped my head between my knees. "No way," I whispered.

If I said it out loud then that made it real.

Shut up, Ellie. Don't say it.

Pregnant.

Maybe.

Swallowing hard, I sat up. Maybe I was just late. Starting a new job was the ultimate form of stress and it could have pushed my cycle into the red zone. Not that I'd ever, ever, *ever* been late in my life, but I could be.

I did some math in my head and it wasn't good. Not good at all. "Damn you, Crescent Cove water."

I rose and stared at myself in the mirror. My face was a bit pale, but otherwise, I looked the same. I'd swapped out my Christmas smock for a Valentine's day one over my skinny jeans and fuzzy sweater.

And now I had to pee.

"Shoot." I hung up my smock and started unbuttoning my jeans. Then I hesitated. Should I hold it for a pee test?

Did I want to get a pregnancy test here?

Everyone would know I'd gotten one. As it was, people still asked me if I had talked to the hot artist from the festival.

The answer was no.

No, I had not, and I didn't intend to.

Not really.

Probably not.

But now?

Quickly, I did my business and washed my hands. I took my smock with me, but I hung it up in our little locker area. I didn't have a customer for another hour. That was just enough time to go to the pharmacy in the next town over.

I really didn't want to be the next bit of gossip fodder in this town.

But if I was pregnant...

The timing was all wrong. The situation was crazy. I wasn't ready to be a mother.

Or was I?

ELEVEN

MY CAR WAS THE CAUSE OF MY LIFE STRESS.

I should sell it.

Burn it?

Nah, too hasty. Selling it was a good idea. To someone far enough away that I would never take the chance of seeing it again on the street. A person in Idaho, for example. I never went to Idaho. That had to be safe.

I even went online and searched for a small town in that state with a dealership that might want to buy back my baby. I was that desperate.

Or insane, take your pick.

I'd stayed up too late grading papers several nights in a row, which had led to a recent dependence on Death by Coffee. Turned out they weren't lying. Once you got on that stuff, it was hard to get off of it.

Who needed sleep, right?

Well, it turned out I did. Since my breakup—did it count as a breakup if our entire relationship had lasted under thirty-six hours?— and the start of the semester had worn me raw, I obviously should not be making big life choices.

So, naturally, I made several.

I didn't sell my car. I did, however, agree to move my appointment

93

for custom work to mid-February. Specifically, February 14th. A day I was guaranteed not to be busy, since I'd been dropped faster than tequila made a woman's clothes come off.

Also, I was never voluntarily listening to the country channel on satellite radio again.

But as that date drew closer and my loneliness grew deeper instead of lessening, I began to consider the paths life had taken me on. Specifically, how I'd ended up in Crescent Cove and when I was going back.

There could be a message that I wasn't seeing.

Sure, certain heartbreak and an early onset midlife crisis seemed like the likely ones. But I was an artist. Trained to look deeper.

An artist who was doing a series of paintings on the one woman I was supposed to be forgetting. So far, that wasn't working out too well. Not to mention I was dreaming about her so much that I had no choice but to get them out of my head and on to paper.

I looked between the trio of canvases I had on easels in my studio. What I should've done was put them up for consignment—once they were finished anyway. The last thing I needed were more reminders of her.

Though it didn't matter, because I thought of her all day every day anyway.

The first one was an amalgamation of that charcoal drawing I'd done in the park the day after our kiss. I'd changed her attire from just the scarf to the white dress shirt I'd dreamed of the night we'd been together. The material draped over her curves, clinging to her in some places and falling loosely in others.

Of course I kept dreaming about her in it.

I was near obsessed with getting everything down. The interesting shadows that teased the juncture of her thighs, mostly hidden by her shirttails. *My* shirttails, the buttons strategically undone. Her long hair dipped over one eye.

She made the perfect ingenue.

Perfectly unattainable.

In the second painting, she was different, although the changes were modest. Her hair was just a bit wilder, her shoulders back, the shirt barely held closed. More shadows. More defiance in every line of her body. Her beauty fisted my throat and made the sweeps of my paintbrush erratic.

I tried to catalog every detail, to show the subtle changes from the first. I didn't know why I'd done a series. We'd only had that one stolen night. It wasn't as if I'd seen her evolve. I never would.

The third canvas was bare.

I didn't know what I'd do for that one. I'd just known I had to do three.

After I'd worked for a while getting the shading just right of her hair over her shoulder, I grabbed my phone and took a few quick snapshots of the paintings in progress. I liked to catalog the stages of each piece. Some of my customers enjoyed seeing the process of them coming to life. And sometimes, I just needed to have a record of every step.

Then I tossed my cell over my shoulder in the direction of the mattress and went back to it.

Awhile later, my phone buzzed, and I fumbled on my bed until I found it in the disordered sheets. When I did manage to lay down, rest was elusive. More nights than not, I stumbled out of bed to paint. I was driven to finish these, even if it felt like I was painting a future I couldn't see yet.

Maybe that was just wishful thinking.

I glanced at the readout. My real estate agent, Connie.

My heartbeat kicked into high gear.

"Hi, Connie. What's up?"

"You know what's up. Your offer was accepted."

I sat on the edge of my bed. "No counter?"

"None. Looks like you're going to be a new homeowner, Callum. Congratulations."

Those words echoed in my head as I drove toward Crescent Cove an hour later. Instead of the mini blizzard I'd encountered the first time I'd driven this route, today the sunshine reflected off the icicles gleaming on roofs and sparkled on the thin glaze of snow on lawns. It was still cold enough to freeze my balls, but the sun made me think spring was coming.

Someday.

Dare had a loaner waiting for me when I dropped off my car for the custom work we'd talked about. He was in the middle of a job so he just waved hello while Gage handled the paperwork.

"I'm going to live here soon," I announced.

Not that he'd asked. Or even spoken much to me. Apparently, Crescent Cove-ites had long memories. At least this one did.

He grunted. "Oh, yeah?"

"Yes, I'm buying a house on the lake."

"Where exactly?"

We discussed details, and surprise of all surprises, Gage was my new neighbor. Sort of. He wasn't right next door, which probably was good for the state of my pumpkins next Halloween. He seemed much friendlier today than he had in December, but I wouldn't exactly say he'd rolled out the welcome wagon.

Closer though. In general, the townsfolk were pretty friendly. Maybe eventually, I'd be one of them.

Dare's idea of a loaner was more family friendly than my sports car. The Jeep was more practical than mine as well, especially to drive out to the lake view roads. I parked on the street near the hair salon and walked straight inside, ready to face my fate with a smile.

All right, that was a total lie. I was already sweating bullets, but I could do a poker face with the best of them. Especially when I had one hell of a bribe in my back pocket.

I hadn't bought a house just to get a woman to go out with me.

Not exactly. That would've been crazy.

I'd done it because the house had spoken to me, as so much of this town did. It was as if I'd been caught in a web once I'd entered the town limits of Crescent Cove. One I didn't want to shake free of anytime soon.

Stepping in to To Dye For made me think of Ellie immediately. Somehow it felt like her. I hadn't been in many salons, but I knew this one with its farmhouse-style décor and plethora of plants was different.

Special. Much like the woman I'd come to whisk away to my house on the water—

No, I'd come to ask her out for a low pressure lunch. I wouldn't scare her away this time. I was living the casual life now.

Minus the offer I'd had accepted on the house she loved. A minor detail, really.

One she didn't need to know about until after lunch. Way after. At least not until I walked her back to her car.

A pretty blond in a billowy poet's blouse flashed a smile at me. "Hi, I'm Paisley. Do you have an appointment?"

"No. I'm actually looking for Ellie."

"Oh. Oh. *Ohhh.*" On the third *oh,* she braced both hands on the counter and actually leaned over to check me out from head to toe. "You must be artist dude. Nice job, girl."

"Excuse me?"

"So, Ellie actually isn't available right now. As you can see." Expansively, she threw back her arm to encompass the rest of the hair styling stations. It was a small operation but had room to grow. Everything was neat as a pin and welcoming. "But you are here. Very much here. Hmm."

"Okay, is she due in today? I can wait. Or maybe you could tell me her hours?"

"No, I can't do that. Confidentiality laws and all."

I frowned. "But this is a salon. What if I wanted her to do my hair?" I swallowed hard at the inappropriate images that filled my head, most of them involving Ellie, shaving cream, and partial nudity.

Perhaps total nudity. It was my daydream. I could make it as X-rated as I wanted to.

As long as I stayed hidden by this counter.

"Hmm, that's an idea, right? I can't send you away if you wanted her to do your *hair.* Since you would be a paying customer and all. No freebies," she added, as if she could sense I was about to demand a chop on the house.

"I'll pay of course."

"Right. Because paying customers have to be served no matter what.

The client is always right. Isn't that true, Melody?" Paisley asked an older blond woman blow-drying a high school-aged girl's hair at the first station. "We have to make sure they're happy."

Melody frowned as she looked between us, and then it appeared as if Paisley did a quick hand gesture just out of my range of sight. "Oh, definitely. The customer is the boss. We just want to make sure they're pleased."

"Right." Paisley nodded vigorously as she faced me again. "So, tell us, what exactly are your needs today?"

I glanced over my shoulder. "Is this going on YouTube? I feel like I'm being videotaped to be made fun of later."

She surprised me by letting out a light laugh. "I like you. You seem responsible." She looked me up and down again. "Nice coat. Burberry? You must have a job."

I took another look at my surroundings. The hidden camera was going to become apparent at any moment, I just knew it. "I do. Two, in fact. One is a bit more…transient, but the other is quite stable. Are you sure Ellie isn't here? I really need to talk to her."

Paisley cocked her head, narrowing her eyes. "Are you going to let her shape your hair? It's overgrown."

"I like it that way," I said defensively.

I didn't add I hadn't gotten it cut since just before I'd met Ellie. Depression tended to do that to a man.

"But yes, she can cut it. She can do whatever she wants to do to me." At Paisley's arched brow, I cleared my throat. "I mean, hair-wise."

"I'm sure."

I stayed silent.

"Good thing Ellie saw you first. Then again, there was a reason she hasn't seen you since. And why might that be?"

I was pretty sure they knew who I was. And that meant Ellie had mentioned me. She hadn't forgotten me the minute she'd rolled out of bed.

Logically, I'd known it wasn't possible. Not after the connection we'd had—and probably still had, if she would just give it a chance.

Somehow I'd have to make her see I was worth the risk.

"It was her choice. I'm here to see if perhaps I can change her mind." I hoped I sounded confident and not overdue for a visit from Sheriff Brooks.

"Is that right?"

"Yes. I'm not here to be a nuisance." God, was I being a fool to do all this? "Look, I just want to see her. I need to see her. I—" I broke off at Paisley's widening smile. "What?"

"Oh, you'll do, won't you? Wait right here while I get her."

I crossed my arms. "I thought you said she wasn't here."

"I said she wasn't available. If you didn't get past the gate, I would've told you that she'd moved to Montana. But you made it past level one. Don't get cocky. You're got many levels to go."

I shook my head as she headed into the back. "This town is always going to keep me on my toes."

"You've got that right," Melody agreed with a wink.

TWELVE

Ellie

"OH, GOOD. THERE YOU ARE." PAISLEY PUSHED ME FARTHER INTO THE back to the room where we did waxing and frowned at me. "Are you okay?"

"I don't know."

She grabbed my hands. "Well, I have some news you may not be excited about. I can get rid of him if you really want me to."

"Rid of who?"

"Hottie artist dude. Your delicious hookup."

I crossed my arms over my middle. "How do you know about Callum?"

"Honey, this is Crescent Cove. Who doesn't know you were kissing a piece of stranger hotness in the park?"

I flushed. Here I'd thought I'd kept a low profile since that day. Little did I know I was still a topic of conversation. "Are people talking about me?"

"Oh, honey. Not like that. We're just all suckers for romance in this town. Especially in the winter. Nothing else happens around here except babymaking, you know that." Paisley frowned. "Are you sure you're all right?"

I didn't know about the rest of her statement, but babymaking was right. Maybe. "Wait, is he here?"

"That's what I was saying. He's out front looking for you."

"Here." I could still breathe, I was almost sure. "In the salon?"

"What else does *here* mean? Are you all right? You look really pale."

I nodded. "Yeah, I'm good."

"I can get rid of him, easy peasy. I'll just dropkick him to the street. He didn't tweak my crazy stalker dude radar, but I've been wrong before."

"No. He's not that. He's been very respectful."

"Not too respectful, I hope." Paisley's smile was wicked. "He looks a bit buttoned up, but seems like maybe not all the way, you know?"

Oh, I knew. He was gentle and sweet, but also I had a memory of him flipping me over and banging the hell out of me on a loop in my dreams. I tried to ignore those particular urges, but if he was here?

And then there was this little lateness thing.

Late.

He was here.

And I could not deal with that right now. No way. "Yeah, get rid of him."

She hooked a thumb toward the front. "Okay. He's dust. Do you want like forever dust or...come back later when I've prettied myself up?"

I touched my hair. "Do I look that bad?"

"No. Of course not. You always look amazing. But you know, a killer 'you can't have this' kind of look. That kind."

I shook my head. I'd tried that before. I'd caved like an overcooked soufflé and ended up going to the festival then losing all my clothes. "I'm not ready to see him. I—"

I'm afraid I might be pregnant, and I can't deal with it on my own, let alone deal with freaking out in front of my possible baby daddy.

Oh, and I had to talk to him here in front of my co-workers. You know, no big deal.

Paisley drew me into her arms and hugged me hard. "It's okay. Whatever it is, it's okay."

My eyes misted, and I leaned into her for a second. I linked my arms around her and hugged her back. "Thanks."

"Us girls gotta stick together."

I nodded. "Okay." I dabbed at my eyes. "Send him back to my chair."

"I'll be right here if you need me." She squeezed my arm one more time and went back to the front.

I believed her. It was a new feeling for me. It remained to be seen just how much I'd need my new friend.

I stopped at the lockers and put on my smock again. I fluffed my hair and detangled my hoops from the fresh highlights Paisley had done for me the day before.

"He's just a guy. You can talk to him and then…" I stared at myself in the mirror.

And then…what?

Then I'd deal with whatever came next. That was what I always did.

Pushing open the curtain, I straightened my shoulders and crossed to my station. I took a minute to soak all of him in. It should have been easier to see him by now.

My gaze tracked down his long, muscular frame. His Burberry coat was open over one of his usual cardigan sweaters. This one was a soft gray like his eyes. His jeans had stress wears in all the right places and a pair of battered Timberlands peeked out from the frayed cuffs. Again, there was an affluence to him that didn't quite match his artist moniker.

I thought most artists made their money posthumously—unless they were in the city. Maybe Syracuse wasn't his home either. Maybe a lot of different things. I didn't really know Callum MacGregor very well.

Well enough to sleep with him.

Well enough to make a baby.

Maybe.

"Ellie?" He stepped closer.

I'd totally zoned out. "Sorry. I'm a bit distracted. Did you want a haircut?" I immediately reached up to sift my fingers through his hair. And I wished I hadn't. I was used to touching because hair was my job.

Callum wasn't just a head of hair.

His cedar and brisk winter air scent set me back on my heels. It dragged me back to the festival and his arms around me.

He leaned into my touch, his eyes closing. "I missed you touching me."

I dropped my hand. "I'm sure you could find another hairdresser a bit closer to you. If you're looking for a discount, the MoneyMaster coupon expired last week."

His smile made me light up inside in a way I'd almost forgotten I could. He had given me that at Christmas. "I can pay full price. Why does everyone think I'm cheap?"

"Because you spend all your dough on hot cars and fancy threads?"

I decided to touch his tweed coat this time. Why, I did not know. It looked soft, and I just wanted to lay my head on it and rest. Not plan or worry or stress for one freaking moment and let someone else take care of me.

Not that he'd offered. Or that he wanted to. Just something about his open, hopeful expression and the fact that he kept coming back for me, time and time again, made me want to trust he'd give me a safe place to land for just a little while.

My mom had left me, but this virtual stranger wanted to be in my world. I couldn't figure out how to handle it, so I kept screwing it up.

And now I might be screwing up a life that wasn't even solely my own if I continued on this path.

"Ellie," he murmured as my chin wobbled. I gripped one of his buttons to keep from letting the tears I didn't know I'd stored up flow. "What is it?"

I didn't look up at his face, just stared at his pearlized button clutched between my fingers. "Can we go somewhere?"

"Sure. Of course." His voice was so gentle and not the least bit judgmental. "Where would you like to go?"

"Not anywhere with a bed," I said a touch too loudly, squeezing my eyes shut at the muffled laugh I heard from behind me.

"Who needs one of those? I've heard Crescent Cove trees are mighty sturdy."

I shook my head, laughing despite my nerves. And embarrassment.

And about fifty other emotions he stirred up in me so easily. No wonder I wanted to flee every time he got too close.

"No beds," he said low enough for my ears only. "Let's go for a ride. In a car," he added for the benefit of my eavesdropping coworkers.

I couldn't exactly blame them. Apparently, Callum and I were big news in town. I didn't know why when it came to that either, but I was beginning to think there were a few things I needed to learn more about.

Swallowing deeply, I looked up at Callum. People too.

"Okay. Let me get my jacket." I turned toward Paisley to ask if it was all right, but she was already waving me off. "Oh, I have Mrs. Bloom coming in."

She waved me off. "I'll take care of her."

"Are you sure?"

"Totally. Get out of here, you crazy kids."

The word *kids* stopped me in my tracks. At least that was a bright side. Just one kid. Maybe.

Then again, Callum had triplets in his family. Was that hereditary? I gazed down at my stomach, nicely hidden by my smock.

Nope, I was not going there. I wasn't a big person. There was no room for…all that.

"Are you okay?" Callum asked, peering over my shoulder as I stared at my belly.

"Yes, I'm fine. One second." I whipped off my smock and returned it to my area before grabbing my jacket.

He was waiting for me by the door, and we walked out to the street where he'd parked in silence. When he motioned to a Jeep instead of his hot yellow car, I did a doubletake. "You sold it? Why? I have good memories of that car."

"Me too." The huskiness of his voice made me curl my fingers into my palms. "But no, I'm just getting some custom work done on it at Dare's shop. He gave me this loaner." He opened the passenger door for me. "What do you think of it?"

"I love Jeeps, but if you get one, I hope you paint it neon green. Normal colors don't seem to suit you."

"They don't?" He sounded inordinately pleased.

"Not anymore. I mean, when I first saw the grandpa sweater—" I couldn't stop from giggling when he poked me in the side. "Very attractive grandpa."

"That's better." He frowned. "How old are you anyway?"

"Twenty-four."

"Whew."

"What about you?"

"Thirty in a few months."

"Did you suddenly think I was barely legal? Little late to worry."

He leaned in and spoke against my temple, ruffling my hair with his deliciously warm breath. "I'd have to take my luck with that sort of sin, since I can't seem to stay away. Now get in."

As I did what he asked, I realized I was shivering—and not from the cold.

My hottie artist hookup was dangerous. Not physically, but in every other possible way.

He didn't tell me where we were going, and I didn't say anything as he drove up one of the side roads that led around the lake.

Until he stopped at a hidden lane called Wolf Hollow Way and signaled to make the turn.

We were near the house. *My* house. I'd never gotten quite this close before because this was a private road surrounded by enough trees to make me think of all the scary movies I was only brave enough to watch with all the lights blazing and a big bucket of popcorn. He veered off and drove into a clearing that opened up near the lake, pulling to a stop close to the water.

I opened my door and stepped out, taking a deep breath of air tinged with the scent of the lake. The sun glistened off the cover of ice, nearly blinding me for the second it took to pull out my sunglasses from my jacket pocket.

"You're going to get arrested for trespassing," I warned instead of all the much nicer things that flitted through my brain.

Like...

How beautiful. Thank you for showing me this. How did you know I needed the water and the sunshine?

He didn't blink as he walked around the Jeep to stand with me. I moved back and he shut my door. Always a gentleman.

I didn't know how to share the sweeter parts of myself with him without being worried that he'd toss them back in my face.

For a moment, he shifted from foot to foot, as if he was weighing what to say. Then he went for broke.

"It's not trespassing when you own the place."

"You…I…what? Here? My favorite spot? Why?"

He turned to me, a smile curving his lips. "Turns out you have amazing taste." He stepped forward and cupped my elbows, his touch easy. "I was supposed to invite you to a nice, casual lunch. Then I was supposed to get a haircut. So far, my day isn't going as I planned at all."

"I think I'm pregnant."

In another situation, watching the color leech from his face might've been funny. Right now, it wasn't. Not at all.

"Say that again."

"I think I'm pregnant. I don't know for sure. I haven't taken a test. I'm just late, and I'm never late—Callum, put me down!" I screeched as he lifted me up in the air, spinning me around so fast I gripped his shoulders to keep from falling. But he held on to me securely, never letting go even when I slid down his body back to the ground.

He pushed my sunglasses on top of my head and cupped my face in his hands. "Can we go find out now?"

His gray eyes were filled with excitement and terror and what seemed like genuine pleasure. "Did you understand what I said? What it means?"

"Yes, I was there that day in health class. When sperm meets egg, you get a baby or babies—"

"Baby. Say it with me. B-a-b-y. As in one, singular. I don't have the capacity for triplets."

"Oh, you'd be surprised how elastic—"

I reached up to close his lips with my fingers. "Unless you want me to talk about how elastic your male body parts are, please don't."

He chuckled and nodded, so I dropped my hand. He immediately grabbed it and lifted it to his mouth to kiss my knuckles. "I was warned about Crescent Cove. I can't say I really believed it, but it didn't stop me from being with you. Nothing would. Not a hurricane or a blizzard or a Dear John note on the dresser when I was already on my way to falling in love with you."

The words spun around dizzily in my head. I stumbled back to lean against the Jeep because the world was tilting, and I wasn't entirely sure it was just because he was a gorgeous, wonderful, insane man.

He moved toward me instantly. "Are you all right? Do you want to sit down? I don't have the keys yet, but there are chairs on the wraparound porch."

I shook my head, pressing my lips together against a smile. Warmth bloomed inside me, the kind that even my logical mind couldn't squash. "I didn't even know the house was for sale."

"Me either. My timing was just right. Guess it was fate."

"Fate or not, you can't fall in love in not even a day. It's not possible."

"Tell that to Ariadne, who fell in love with Theseus as soon as she saw him on the dock, which probably isn't that dissimilar from a gazebo —why are you laughing?"

"I don't know who those people are."

"They're from Greek mythology. I teach it at the community college. It's not as fancy a position as Lennox has with his powerful law firm, or Finn with his architectural firm, but it suits me. I'm a good teacher." Not so subtly, he moved closer to me. "I have patience and a love of the subject material."

"You have good hands too," I mused idly as he cupped my hips. Then I laughed again, feeling like the hugest fool who had ever lived. "You're really a professor? I thought you were a flighty artist with an inconsistent income."

"I really am a professor. And I can be flighty. And my income can be inconsistent, though less so in the past couple of years thanks to my paintings." He rubbed his thumb over my lower lip. "But I'm exceptional at making promises. I don't give my word unless I can keep it."

"Callum," I whispered, but I wasn't strong enough to hold him off.

Not when I so badly wanted him to line up our mouths and kiss me like he'd missed me so much over the past six weeks. Just as I'd missed him.

He slid his fingers through my windswept hair, his lips gentle and persuasive with that undercurrent of need that had me rising to my tiptoes to meet his kiss. I wound my arms around his waist, nestling them under his long coat, and just allowed myself to sink into him. To enjoy for a moment without thinking about the next.

Breathless, we finally parted a few minutes later. He ran his fingertip between my breasts and kept on going, stopping just above my belly button. "Do you really think so?"

The wonder in his question made a lump form in my throat. "It's a definite possibility."

"If you are, if *we* are, I'll do everything in this world to make you happy. I swear it on my life." His Adam's apple bobbed. "I'll make both of you happy and me too. Or you know, all four of us—" He laughed as I punched him in the ribs. "Ow. My woman is strong."

"Is that what I am?" I was still dazed from all he'd said.

Words were easy. Emotions and actions weren't. And if he was faking his reaction to the possible existence of this child, then he had me fooled. His sincerity was as much a part of him as his cedar scent or the misty gray of his eyes.

Or his sweet, confusing heart.

He drew me against him and brushed my hair off my cheek. "If you'll have me."

"I'm scared." Admitting it was probably the hardest thing I'd ever done.

"Oh, baby, I am too." He pressed my hand against his chest so that I could feel his rapid heartbeat through the material. "But it's a good scared. It means I want this. I want you and what can be. Whatever is meant for us. I'm right here, ready to take every step with you."

My lips quivered into a smile as I put my sunglasses back into place. "Is that casual lunch still on the table? Because suddenly, I'm starving."

I wasn't lying. For the first time in a while, all I wanted was a big juicy cheeseburger and thick steak fries from the diner. Or that poutine from Gina that Paisley had mentioned.

And if some of the reason my appetite had returned was because of this impossible, incredible man beside me, well, so be it.

I wasn't running anymore.

"Absolutely. Your choice. Let's go." He started walking around the Jeep to the driver's side, but I grabbed his hand and held on tight as he looked back at me.

"After we go buy a pregnancy test? If you wouldn't mind being there while I make sure."

This time, I wasn't even surprised when he spun me around. Although I made him put me down a lot faster, since my stomach and I weren't on the best of terms when he tried stuff like that.

But the rest of me secretly loved it.

God, I was a sap.

The whole way to the drugstore a town over, Callum rubbed my knee and smiled at me every time our gazes locked. Which was often.

When I'd told him where to go, he hadn't even questioned why we had to travel so far when there were stores in town.

And when I went in the store's small, dingy bathroom to do what I needed to do, he paced in the hallway, asking every thirty seconds, "Is it time yet?"

I opened the door and took a quick glance around before dragging him inside so he could look at the little stick with me.

One of us whooped. It was probably him. I was too shell-shocked to do anything but press my forehead against his strong, solid chest when he hauled me into a hug.

"We did it," he murmured into my hair over and over.

I let out a sniffly laugh. "You do realize this wasn't a goal we were aiming for. It just kind of happened."

"Yes, we got lucky. It's as if we're in our own mythology tale, centered in that far away land called Crescendia Cove. They'll write about us someday."

As I laughed harder, he smoothed his thumbs under my cheeks. That was how I knew I was crying. "Is that so?"

"Yes. The story will be about the beautiful woman with pink messy braids and hope in her eyes who kissed the lonely man under the mistletoe and gave him a reason to believe. And he pledged to give her and their baby a lifetime of Christmases, because who says you can only celebrate once a year?"

I leaned against him, because I was finally beginning to have faith that I could. That he wouldn't have come back so many times if he didn't truly want to stay.

"Who says," I repeated softly as his lips met mine.

Epilogue

ELLIE

Christmas Eve Eve

MY BREATH CAUGHT ON THE TURN INTO MY HOUSE. *OUR* HOUSE—A HOUSE made for a family. Something I'd never dreamed of having. Cal had indulged me in my love of Christmas decorations. I was pretty sure he might be out-Christmasing even me.

The huge oak tree at the edge of our property was decked out in about a bazillion white lights. Huge red Christmas balls and illuminated white stars swung merrily in the breeze off the water. Callum had spent one of the nice Sundays in November monkeying all over that tree to get it done. All because he found a photo in my family look book.

Well, it was sort of ours now.

Photos for inspiration that I'd found in magazines and printed out from online made up the book, just like with my hair-focused one. I knew Pinterest would be easier, but it had seemed to be the perfect joint planning thing for us as we'd gotten to know each other over the last year. He sneaked in sketches, and I went for glossy photos.

His brothers—who were just as insane as he'd warned me—had

come to help decorate while his mom and I stayed on a quilt with the babies.

Yeah, babies. Plural.

Wouldn't have pegged me spending my pregnancy bonding with my mother-in-law-to-be through thick ankles, stretch marks, and late night cravings, but I had. Cal had gotten the news that his mother was pregnant a day after we'd taken our test. We'd gone to tell his folks, and they'd had a special update of their own.

Cal and his dad had worn matching stunned expressions for a few weeks.

His mom had given birth to Cal early in life, and while she wasn't the oldest mother in the medical journals, she'd astounded our obstetrician with how easily she'd made it through the pregnancy. I guessed after triplets, anything was easy. And because I didn't have a doctor of my own, we'd just ended up doing our entire pregnancies together, right down to the office visits.

But my fiancé had a master's degree in adapting. He happened to have one in Mythology as well. If he ever finished his thesis for his PhD, he'd be a full-fledged doctor too.

But our new little family kept him busy.

Our deep and abiding love for this crazy Victorian house on the lake took up even more time. Cal had made it his mission in life to make all my dreams come true. It was a bit more of a fixer upper than we'd been expecting. There had been a reason the sellers had taken his offer with no questions asked. We'd been renovating it during the majority of my pregnancy, but we were taking a break to enjoy our new little girl's first year.

That and our daughter had inherited my allergy to plaster dust.

It was just too much misery for one man to take.

The farther I got up the drive, the more I was able to let the stress of the day fade. The salon had been madness. We'd hired two more stylists and a barber. With the unending beard love, men were looking to up their salon game, and we were happy to move with the times.

Going back to work had been hard, but knowing our daughter was in good hands—mostly her dad's—had made it a little easier to go back part-time. Cal was done with school for the holidays and had decided to bring his class load down to two classes in the new semester.

Painting was taking up more and more of his time. And he liked being home with our baby. She was such a daddy's girl, she'd probably have a paintbrush in her hands before a crayon. I was okay with it, especially because Cal was just as wrapped around her little finger as I was.

We were spending Christmas Day at the MacGregor farm so we were keeping Christmas Eve for ourselves. I still had a million things to do. I'd been perfecting my lasagna game on Cal's brothers for the last two weeks. I was pretty sure the last batch in my passenger seat was going to knock my fiancé's socks off.

It wasn't that I was a bad cook, I was just very regimented. It wasn't fun for me. I could create any color in the rainbow on a head of hair, but ask me to be creative with ingredients and I froze. Luckily, Callum was a decent cook and even better at ordering take-out.

But it was our first official Christmas together, and I really wanted it to be special. And naked was definitely on the menu for dessert. Especially since our little insomniac had finally learned how to sleep through the night.

Mostly.

I pulled in the circular drive to my spot. A garage was in the future plans, but for now, we still parked outside. Cal's Supra was tarped and tucked under our carport waiting for spring. He'd wanted to sell it when I'd told him we were pregnant, but I secretly loved that stupid penis mobile.

Surprisingly, his SUV wasn't here. He must have taken the baby out to do some last-minute shopping.

I grabbed the insulated bag that held my precious lasagna and headed for the front steps. I still couldn't believe this was our place. I'd managed to get those traditional bulbs for the roofline in the sale of the house. I mean, really, what was the previous owner going to do with them? It was like they were made for the house.

Each bulb was tucked perfectly into the gingerbread lace along the gables and roofline, as well as the trim and corbels. I'd done a staggering amount of research to make sure any outside renovations kept up with the age of the house. Callum had gotten into the deep dive of research—way past me. The professor in him geeked out and found levels of history to our house I didn't even know how to find.

Then he'd done a painting of the house with me on the porch wearing his white dress shirt for my birthday. He could be very sweet at times. I had a feeling he was working on something else for Christmas. He hadn't let me in his studio for the last few weeks.

Just as I got to the steps, twin beams of light came up the drive. Cal's Mazda SUV slowed around our circular drive. He waved at me then parked.

I set the lasagna down on the steps and went to meet him.

He hopped out and I got a little zing. I wasn't sure I'd ever get used to how sexy my guy was. He had a gray tweed jacket on over a soft black cashmere sweater and jeans. To accent his professor chic, he was wearing his pageboy hat. It shouldn't have worked, but I had one hot teacher-slash-artist for a lover. And soon-to-be husband.

"Hey there. I was hoping I'd beat you home." He drew me in for a quick kiss.

"Well, hello there yourself. You taste like…chocolate."

There were enough lights on our house to light up a street so I could plainly see the flush rising up his neck. "I had to pick up a few last-minute presents. Faith and I had a date at the diner."

"You had Greta's chocolate cream pie, didn't you?"

He held up a finger. "I did. But…" He leaned back into the SUV and pulled out a bag. "I brought a whole pie home for Christmas."

"Okay. Forgiven." I took the bag and peeked inside. "Anything else for me in there?"

"Different bag and not until tomorrow."

"Mean."

He grinned at me. Then the piercing scream of our daughter tried to shatter glass. He crossed his eyes and put his other bags down. He opened the door to the backseat. "Faith Mistletoe MacGregor, what is your malfunction?"

I laughed and peeked around the window to wiggle my fingers at Faith. "Hello, love. Are you giving your daddy trouble?"

"Only because she's not the center of attention for five seconds."

Faith giggled and grabbed Cal's beard.

"Ouch." He untwisted her fingers and finally got the five point harness undone. Just like a champ, he had her swaddled into the blanket we always kept in the car. Coats and carseats didn't work anymore with all the new laws.

I flipped back the edge of the blanket so she could see me. "Boo."

Faith's laugh bubbled out along with some drool. I had a feeling teething was going to be in our future sooner rather than later. Cal hiked her onto his shoulder and grabbed her bag, handing it off to me.

Weighed down with all our bags, we trudged up to the front steps.

"What's this?" He pointed at the insulated container on the porch.

"Nothing."

"Hmm." He gave me a narrow-eyed look and opened the door for me.

Before I could get through the door, he gave me a quick, hot kiss.

He glanced up at the mistletoe.

"That's new." I couldn't stop the smile even as Faith howled out her disgust at being bundled up.

"Okay, okay. I'm moving as fast as I can." We headed inside and Cal whipped off her blanket and slung it on the couch. "I may have put a few decorations up."

I automatically picked up the blanket and folded it. "We have decorations everywhere."

"Yeah, just a few." He bounced Faith a few times to get her giggling again as he undid her sweater.

I glanced at the archways to each room from the foyer. There were lit up bows of evergreen tacked up with a little dangling bit of mistletoe for each. "Really?"

"What? It's the Christmas spirit."

"You don't need an excuse to kiss me, sir."

"No, but I don't mind the extra bonus kisses." He picked up two of the shopping bags and dropped them by the tree.

I followed, picking up the baby things he'd left laying around. Before we got into the kitchen, he swung me around into his arms with Faith. He planted a kiss on Faith's ruddy cheeks then one on my laughing mouth.

"Did you eat?" He went right for the fridge and took out a bottle for Faith. We had a nice schedule down for her, and it seemed to help her sleeping habits.

Callum was a very good father. Between the research he'd done—books on baby to childhood development littered our bedroom and another dozen were scattered in his office—and his precise schedule, we had a damn happy baby on our hands.

And a happy mom. I didn't worry about leaving him alone with her. Callum had stepped up and then some. His studio was a study in chaos, but when it came to our baby, he was as organized as...well, a teacher.

Guess I'd gotten the best of both worlds there.

I picked up the cap from the bottle and put it in the sterilizer. Well, some things were still chaos. And personally, the fact that he wasn't perfect was a relief. I certainly wasn't.

He'd settled with the baby at the kitchen table. He propped up her bottle with his thumb and took off his hat, tossing it on the table. "Did you want to feed her?"

I moved to kiss her goose-down fluffy blond curls then threaded my fingers through his wild hat hair. "Nah, you guys are all settled. I'll just put some stuff away."

He snagged the loop on my jeans and dragged me back. He lifted his chin toward the holly berries mixed with mistletoe hanging from the chandelier. "Pay your toll first."

I bent down and kissed him softly. "How many of these do you have in the house?"

"A few."

I rolled my eyes, but I had a feeling I'd enjoy the hunt after Faith went to bed.

Domestic chores took up the rest of our evening. Laundry, bath time, and Callum's favorite part of the night—story time.

I looked in on them in the rocking chair in Faith's room. It was one of the smaller rooms in the house, but right next door to ours. It was painted a soft lavender with ash furniture in a pale sandy color. We'd put up a small pre-lit tree in her room on her dresser. There was an ornament from each of her uncles hanging up, as well as her grandma and grandpa. Even her new aunt Cara had sent an ornament for her tree.

New traditions—just for our little family.

It was pretty amazing.

I was happy to see there was no mistletoe in her room. It was poisonous, after all. And knowing Cal, all the mistletoe in the house was probably silk, just to be safe.

But Faith was definitely in the 'put everything in her mouth' phase. Right now, it was the corner of her Llama Lovey's tail from Paisley. I watched them for a little while longer then sneaked away to shower off the day.

When I returned to our room, the lights were turned on low, and candles were flickering all over the room. The Christmas tree was lit up in our triple window, and the fireplace was crackling. I expected Cal to be lounging on the bed waiting for me, but the room was empty.

In the corner, just beyond the tree, was one of Cal's easels.

Did I know him or what?

A canvas was wrapped in kraft paper with a massive red bow.

There was something different about the room. I looked around, and finally landed on the paintings over our headboard. There was usually three hung up there. The triptych Cal had painted of me. I still wasn't used to seeing my form on a canvas, but I was getting used to seeing myself through his eyes.

The first painting was the altered version of his drawing with my red scarf. Now I was wearing a man's white dress shirt, teasing innocence and a hint of all the curves he loved to draw.

The second painting was a bit more wild. My hair looked as if I'd just spent the night making love. Instead of being buttoned, this shirt showed more than it hid, and my chin was lifted, my eyes defiant and hooded with knowledge.

The third was softer. I was rounder with my baby-filled belly peeking from the shirt. The cuffs were rolled up, and my engagement ring sparkled on my left hand.

I glanced down at my ring and thumbed the underside of the band to straighten it. The icy diamond was in an antique setting with a starburst shape of smaller diamonds surrounding it. Callum never did anything small.

A hand slid along my hip. Cal's cedar scent surrounded me just before his arms did. His slightly rough fingers slipped inside my robe to trace over my waist. "Our princess is finally asleep."

"Must have been right after I left. You've been busy."

"I pulled out most of the stuff earlier. Just stashed it in the closet." He kissed my neck. "I know we have tomorrow as our day with Faith, but I couldn't wait any longer to give you your present."

I covered his hand with my left one. "I've been thinking about yours too."

He tucked his chin on my shoulder. "Oh? Is it under this robe?"

"Kinda."

He toyed with the sash. "I like the idea of that."

I turned in his arms. "You're easy to please."

"You naked is pretty much my favorite amusement park."

I laughed as I cupped his cheek. "I love you, Cal."

He straightened up a little and caught my wrist. He swallowed thickly. "You don't say it a lot, but I know you do."

"Saying it isn't easy for me, but this past year has shown me what it's like to love. I'm so grateful for you and our little girl. And that you've given me so much time and patience to figure it out."

He dropped a light kiss on my lips. "You're worth waiting for. Besides, I've got a ring on it." He brushed his nose along mine. "I know you're not going anywhere."

"How about we put another ring on? You too, this time."

A smile spread across his face. "Are you asking me to marry you? Didn't we already do that?" He picked up my left hand and kissed my ring.

"Yeah, but I think we should do the real deal. The ceremony and the family, the dress and all the crazy that goes with it. Though I'm thinking more of a small thing. Maybe in our backyard in front of the lake."

"Yeah?" He cleared his throat. "I could get behind that."

"I'd say Valentine's Day, but it might be a little chilly. So, how does May sound to you?"

"I say it sounds like a damn fine Christmas present. Do I get to show you mine now?"

"Could it be on the easel?"

"Maybe." He flicked the tail of my robe. "Might want to close that though, or I'll never get through the unwrapping, because I enjoy unwrapping you way more."

I cinched my belt and followed him to the tree. I touched the tip of a mockingbird ornament I'd found in Kinleigh's shop. She always had the best ornaments. I'd never really had a reason to buy them until now.

Cal grabbed my hand and dragged me over to the easel. "Okay, open it."

"No ceremony or ritual this time?"

"No. Just nerves."

I hooked my finger around his pinky. "I always love your paintings."

"I know. Just I worked hard on them."

"Them?" I moved in front of the easel and carefully untied the ribbons from the corner. I laid the long streamers and carefully constructed bow on the chair in the corner. Then I pulled the washi tape from the back of the package. It was so lovingly wrapped that I had a feeling I shouldn't rip into it.

Even if my guy's impatience practically vibrated through the room.

But I was rewarded for the careful attention. On the inside of the kraft paper were little pencil drawings of Faith and I through the last few months. Me breast feeding her, us going for a walk around the lake, Faith sleeping on her daddy's desk, and even a few of her nestled in blankets on his dropcloths.

I laid the little treasures on our bed. Those would be going in my family book.

I went back to the painting and peeled back the muslin covering. My heart tripped out of my chest at the soft focus portrait. Callum's beloved white dress shirt had another starring role. This time, our daughter was cradled in my arms. My hair was gathered on top of my head, with a few tendrils teasing my neck and cheeks.

Faith's newborn face was pink and healthy and full of serenity as she gazed up at me.

"Is this what you see?"

"Every time."

My eyes misted as I touched Faith's sweet face and the absolute awe on mine. "It's beautiful, Cal. One of the most beautiful things I've ever seen."

"I'm glad. The two loves of my life right there." He came up behind me. "And a little something extra back there too."

I lifted the canvas off the easel and found another painting. It was larger and more square. I tugged away the covering and laughed. "That's so perfect."

The white shirt was pooled around Faith and a mass of Christmas lights on top of a pile of dropcloths. She was on her tummy and had the corner of the shirt collar in her mouth.

"I figure we can have this less intimate painting for the downstairs." He pressed the side of his cheek against mine. "A little painting history of our mistletoe baby every Christmas sounds like a perfect holiday tradition."

I spotted the tiny sprig of mistletoe in the corner of the painting with Cal's signature.

"Our mistletoe baby. I like the sound of that."

"So, what's next? A firecracker baby?"

I spun around and wrapped my arms around his neck. "What happens if the next baby is conceived on a Wednesday?"

"So, you do want a next baby?"

I shrugged. "Maybe. And I guess a firecracker baby sounds good to me too."

"And maybe a Valentine's Day heart?"

"Don't push your luck."

He grinned. "I'm never going to stop doing that."

Thanks for reading **MISTLETOE BABY!**
We appreciate our readers so much!
If you loved the book please let your friends know.
If you're so inclined, we'd love a review on your favorite book site.

Looking for more holiday fun?
All we had was one seductive night, New Year's Eve. No names. No phone numbers. No second chances. Then I accidentally ended up working as his nanny…and I just found out I'm pregnant.

Turn the page for a special sneak peek of
CEO DADDY - a Crescent Cove standalone.

CEO DADDY

I might be single and alone on New Year's Eve. But I'm not woe is me. No, ma'am. I'm looking at this moment as an opportunity to cherish my solitude.

WITH A SIGH, I SET DOWN MY PEN AND PICKED UP MY WATER GLASS. I should be drinking alcohol at least. Maybe I still would. I wasn't much of a wine fan, but I could use tonight to broaden my horizons. A cocktail sounded nice. Very adult.

A drink I could enjoy happily on my own.

Okay, cut the crap. In my diary, I should be honest. The diary I was writing in while I ate my dinner of consommé—fancy soup essentially—and garlic breadsticks, because who was I going to kiss at midnight? No one.

Joyfully solo, that was me.

In reality, I was fresh off another broken Tinder date. Broken by *me*, no less. I could never quite close the deal. Probably because a date with me held more weight than the usual hookup.

I'd been adult about that too. Virginity was a burden, so I'd just rid myself of it quickly and quietly. No fuss. Until the time came to actually meet Joe Blow in the flesh—yes, that was his name on the site—and I'd balked. I'd made up an excuse about getting together with an ex and that had been that.

As if I had any exes. Just a few high school boyfriends who hadn't amounted to much.

Since then, I'd stuck close to home, the dutiful older sister who raised her younger siblings after our parents had died in a plane crash. Now that the twins, Emma and Rachel, had turned nineteen and gone off to college, that left me at loose ends.

Alone for real.

"Can I get you anything else? Maybe you'd like a look-see at the dessert menu? The lemon bars are my favorite. They're my mama's recipe."

I blinked up at the grinning blond waitress. At least I thought she was a waitress, though she had a more commanding air about her despite her small town friendliness. "Your mama works here too?"

"Not anymore. She used to own the joint. Then she retired and sold it out from under me with no warning, but I got it back because of my lovable pain-in-the-ass baby daddy. Well, husband too. So, lemon bars?"

I rubbed my temple. Whoa, information overload. "You have a husband? You look...youthful."

Luckily, I'd managed not to say she looked twelve, which was a misstatement in any case. She looked at least sixteen. But not old enough to be married, at least in New York.

She laughed and sat down opposite me at the table. "Sure do."

"And a baby."

"Yeah, she's not even a year old yet. Star's the light of my life. Want to see?" She was already tugging a folding wallet of pictures—many, many pictures—out of her apron pocket.

"Um, sure?"

She showed me an array of photos of a chubby baby with bright green eyes and a drooly smile.

"She's beautiful. Her hair is so dark."

"Like Oliver's. Unless it changes. I hope it doesn't. It's my ace in the hole I wasn't impregnated by the milkman."

Unsure if she was serious, I smiled faintly. "I think I'll try those lemon bars, please."

She nodded enthusiastically and bustled off to the kitchen. She seemed sweet.

Everyone in Crescent Cove was sweet. It was a picturesque village, nestled against the long curve of Crescent Lake. At the holidays, the place really shone.

The big formal banquet room I was seated in was jammed with guests. Most were families, along with a good amount of couples and solo businessmen passing through the area due to the proximity to Syracuse. I lived in between Crescent Cove and Syracuse, in a town so tiny you could miss it if you shut your eyes.

Which you shouldn't do while driving, especially in the fall and winter. We were in deer and wild turkey country.

Spending New Year's Eve in Crescent Cove was a luxury. I didn't have the funds to spare on such things, but I'd asked for money for Christmas from my sisters and my bestie just so I could splurge.

Now I was wondering if it was a huge mistake.

I'd thought I would feel less on my own in a crowd.

Wrong.

I'd had to wait a half hour for this table. There was holiday music playing, and cheerful lights twinkling, and every surface seemed to be decked out with candles and poinsettias and big satin red ribbons. People were laughing and enjoying time with their loved ones.

And I was scribbling lies in my diary about how I didn't mind that my sisters had chosen to return to campus early rather than hang out with their big sister. That I wasn't at all jealous my bestie had a date for New Year's with a guy she worked with.

Worst of all? The prospect of homemade lemon bars excited me more than the gorgeous fireplace suite I'd reserved to spend the evening —you guessed it—alone.

"Here you go. I gave you an extra one. On holidays, calories don't count." The blond proprietress smiled and set the plate in front of me. "Can I get you anything else?"

"Yes, actually, you can. I'd like some champagne, please."

"Oh, sure." She nodded as if it wasn't weird at all I was ordering champagne with lemon bars after drinking water since I'd sat down. "Flute or bottle for the table?"

Did she know something I didn't? Was it usual for women dining alone to drink a whole bottle of bubbly? Maybe on New Year's Eve, anything went.

"Bottle for the table, please." The deep voice barely registered. In fact, I didn't even look to see the owner. He couldn't be speaking for my table. I definitely didn't know anyone who sounded like *that*.

Hello, man, not a boy.

The blond shifted away from me and I dazedly followed her gaze to where one of the businessmen I'd noticed earlier stood beside the chair opposite me. I hadn't seen his face, just the tidy queue of dark hair on his neck as he was seated. A solo diner, just like me.

Unlike me, he hadn't been writing in a journal with flowers on the tattered cover. No, he'd been flipping through a thick sheaf of paperwork, and he'd barely looked up long enough to order.

I hadn't seen his face, but he'd seen mine. Or else he was in the habit of joining strangers once the alcohol was served. Judging by his well-cut pinstriped dark suit and fancy Italian leather briefcase, he wasn't hurting for money. I preferred looking at those things rather than his features. If his looks matched up with his voice—

Well, let's just say I wasn't in any shape to handle that level of disappointment once he rethought his decision. Because, seriously? Why did he want to sit with *me*?

"Oh." The blond smiled. "Are you joining her?" She glanced at me. "Dinner date?"

Normally, the blond's presumptuousness might have irritated me, but it felt as if she was on my side. Like she was making sure I wanted this guy to sit at my table. I must be giving off vibes that I did *not* know this dude. No matter how handsome he was and how important he seemed, a woman had to be careful.

"Two people eating alone on New Year's Eve should eat together." His deep voice caused a tingle low in my belly. "Sage, you know I'm harmless." His smile was anything but.

The blond—Sage—raised an eyebrow. "So said Ted Bundy." She smiled sweetly and shifted to glance at me. "Your call."

He switched his briefcase to the other hand, allowing me to see the bundle of winter tulips he also held, wrapped with a burlap bow and with pine greenery overflowing the colorful tissue paper. Tulips were a weakness of mine, and I'd never seen a winter bouquet of them before.

As if he'd noticed me staring at them, he held them out as additional incentive. "For you."

I borrowed a page from Sage's book and lifted an eyebrow, saying nothing. But I accepted the flowers. I was no dummy, and the tulips were gorgeous. I could already imagine them in the center of my table at home, cheering me up as I experimented in the kitchen. The pale reds, pinks, and yellows were perfect.

"He can sit."

Sage nodded. "Would you like anything else besides the bottle of champagne?"

"A cup of coffee for me, please." His smile was easy and self-assured, and he never looked away from me as he took the seat opposite me at the table.

Sage left us alone with a waggle of her brows.

"Friend of yours?" I set the bouquet of tulips in my lap and drew a nail through the powdered sugar beneath the lemon bars on my plate. I rued not redoing my nail polish for tonight. The silver was chipped at the edges. Surely, a man like him would notice.

"Oh, Sage? No, not exactly, although we've met a few times. I make it a point to eat here when I'm in town. Something I'll be doing a lot more soon."

He paused as Sage brought over the bottle of champagne and two glasses. She popped the cork and poured for us both, then left us alone again. A moment later, she brought his coffee, which he largely ignored.

I picked up my glass, clinked with my new dinner guest, and sipped.

The bubbly went straight to my head as it always did, so I set the glass down.

He was still watching me, his lips curved ever so slightly. He hadn't taken a drink yet.

"I'm Asher," he said as the silence extended uncomfortably. Somehow our personal silence was much more noticeable because of all the excited chatter around us.

"Hannah."

"Nice to meet you. What brings you here tonight of all nights?"

"I didn't want to sit alone at home." *Nice one, Hannah. Can you sound any more pathetic?* "It's a night for parties and fun." I saluted him with my champagne and drank.

Heat flowed out from my belly through my limbs. I couldn't decide if I liked the sensation or not. Or maybe the heat was from Asher's gaze. His eyes weren't as dark as I'd originally believed. With the candle flickering between us, I'd guess now they were a warm hazel, perhaps varying depending on his clothing.

Apparently, his black pinstriped suit didn't offer any appreciable change to them. But whoa nelly, that suit was working wonders on me.

Maybe three-piece suits really were the equivalent to lingerie for a woman. His was definitely revving my motor.

Revving everything.

"So, do you have plans after this? A party perhaps, or some other kind of fun?" He ran his fingertip along the rim of his glass.

"How old are you?" I blurted.

His dark brows drew together. "Thirty-two in March."

"Hmm."

"Is that a good *hmm* or a bad *hmm*?"

"I'm twenty-three. I've never..." I took a deep breath. *Try not to embarrass yourself again.* "Well, this is just sharing some lemon bars and champagne, right?"

"That's up to you. Why don't we start with some conversation and go from there?" His slow smile only served to stir me up even more.

Relax in this gorgeous, commanding man's presence? Not likely.

"Sure. Let's begin with why you came over to my table." I picked up my dessert fork and cut off the corner of one of my lemon bars, belatedly remembering he didn't have one. Sage hadn't brought over another plate.

By accident or design? Even without knowing her well, I could easily see her as the matchmaking type.

"Sorry, it's rude of me to eat when you don't have anything. Here." I set down the fork and lifted the plate toward him, swallowing deeply as he pushed aside the vase and the flickering candle to make room for the plate between us.

"We can share." His fingers brushed mine as he broke off a corner and lifted it to his mouth.

His perfect mouth. His lips were neither too full or too sparse. Just right.

As everything he possessed seemed to be. And I hadn't even gotten a look at him beneath the waist.

Probably good. I didn't need to be any more intimidated, especially by pinstriped thirty-two-year-old cocks. I was already freaked out enough.

Hello, out of my league.

"No fork?" I asked a little breathlessly. He seemed the fork-and-knife-at-all-times type to me.

"Nah. Fingers are better. See?" He broke off another piece and lifted it across the table to me, not dropping so much as a crumb. "Lean forward."

I obliged him and his fingertips brushed my lips as he fed me the treat. His voice was entrancing. I was afraid to imagine all the things he could make me do with just one of those husky commands.

His eyes held me in his thrall so completely that I barely noticed the burst of lemon as I swallowed. The bars were a delicious mix of sweet and tart, but I probably wouldn't have noticed if the dessert had been undercooked and bland.

"Good?"

I nodded and he repeated the move several more times. He wasn't even eating himself, just feeding me. He had long, elegant fingers with a surprising bit of ink swirling down his hands. The bold Roman numerals and heavy, old typeface of a latin phrase were mixed with a bit of artistry.

So incongruous to the buttoned-up businessman. It somehow made him even hotter.

Once, out of the corner of my eye, I noticed Sage start to approach with the bill in hand. She took in what was occurring at our shadowy table, widened her eyes, and sped off in the opposite direction.

I would've laughed had I not been so turned on that I could barely think.

What was happening here? We weren't even talking. Was this what occurred when under the influence of a lonely holiday meant for couples and some expensive champagne? I'd had a couple more sips in between rounds of Asher feeding me. Big, bolstering sips. The kind that made a normally shy, awkward woman feel bold.

"No ring," I said casually—or so I hoped. I'd had plenty of time to see his hand as it came closer to my mouth. "You're single?"

"Very. The kind of single that means I'm alone on New Year's Eve, just as you are." He lifted his thumb to his lips and licked off a stray crumb from the piece he'd just fed me. The movement was far more sensual than it had any right to be. "You are alone tonight, aren't you, Hannah?"

Something about the question and his use of my name made my throat tighten to the point that if I hadn't gulped more champagne, I might've choked. This time, I didn't mind the floaty feeling that overtook my body, or the resulting wave of warmth.

"I'm alone far too much these days. But right now? No. Neither of us is alone."

He nodded, lowering his head for an instant while his jaw locked. He finally took a few sips of coffee before he met my gaze once again. "I have a room upstairs. Just for tonight."

Questions flitted through my mind.

Who are you, Asher?

Why did you pick me to talk to?

Was it just that I looked lonely, so I must be an easy target for sexual advances?

In the end, I didn't really care. We were both alone, and no one was waiting for me at home. What did it matter if I chose this handsome man to spend the evening with? No one would be hurt. And I would finally be able to cross one thing off my bucket list.

Sex with a gorgeous man, check.

Sex, period.

But that didn't mean I'd make it easy on him.

"Who were the flowers for?" I stroked the downy soft petals of the pink tulip on top of the bouquet in my lap.

"My grandmother." He smiled wryly. "She thinks I need to get out more, so she'll approve that I gave them to the most beautiful woman I've seen since..." He trailed off, looking uncharacteristically unsure. Even with only knowing him a very short while, I was quite certain Asher rarely faltered. "Ever."

"I believe you don't get out much after that statement." I rested my cheek on my fist. "My hair isn't really blond, by the way. I put in a rinse today. Truth in advertising and all that."

"It doesn't look blond. Not exactly. More like the color of honey." His voice deepened. "Rich and luxurious."

"Glorious Tones hair color thanks you for your appreciation of their product." I toyed with the stem of my now nearly empty champagne glass. "When is the last time you approached a woman with that line about having a room upstairs?"

"Never. I've never had a room upstairs here before." His lips twitched. "And to be honest, I don't have one now. I wasn't planning on staying until I saw you. Writing so furiously in that." He nodded to my abandoned journal. "What were you writing?"

"Where were you going after this?" I countered.

"To my grandmother's. She was going to be who I counted down to midnight with." He finally reached for his champagne and took a single sip. Easing back in his chair, he licked his lips, slowly and surely. "I'd much rather kiss you once the ball drops."

"Which balls are we referring to?"

I didn't know if he'd find me funny or crude. It was usually half and half, depending on my company. But his laughter was quick and appreciative. "You're different than I expected."

"Oh, really? What did you expect? A meek little mouse who'd trot after you and hop right into bed?" Okay, this had to be the champagne talking, because this was next level, even for me.

"No. I wasn't even thinking about bed when I came over here. I just wanted to hear your voice. To see if you ever smiled. You still haven't, you know. Not at me."

"Smiles are earned. Keep trying. You might get there."

"Luckily, I don't give up easily. Why are you alone tonight? No family?"

"No." The lie came easily, and sometimes seemed far too true when my sisters were busy with school and out of touch. My family was a fraction of what it had once been. "Let's just say I live an isolated existence."

It wasn't that far from reality. I was alone too often.

I couldn't stand another moment of it.

"No lover." The word dripped off his tongue, laced with a sensuality that was far beyond my realm of experience.

"No." I tilted my head. "So, what's your story?"

His lips lifted on one side. "I'm a man who works far too much and spends New Year's Eve with his grandmother. What more do you need to know?"

Indeed.

I nodded at the bottle of champagne. "Think we can get that to go?"

Now Available
For more information go to www.tarynquinn.com

CRESCENT COVE CHARACTER CHART

BEWARE...SPOILERS APLENTY IN THIS CHARACTER
CHART. READ AT YOUR OWN RISK!

Ally Lawrence:
Married to Seth Hamilton, mother of Alexander, stepmother of Laurie, best friends with Sage Evans

Andrea Maria Fortuna Dixon Newman:
Mother of Veronica 'Vee' Dixon

Annie Beck:
Married to George Beck, mother of August, Caleb, and Ivy, grandmother of Rhiannon and Vivian

April Finley: Executive assistant to Preston Shaw
Friends with Ryan Moon and Luna Hastings

Arthur Maitland: Real estate developer

Asher Wainwright: CEO Wainwright Publishing
Married to Hannah Jacobs, father of Lily and Rose

August Beck: Owns Beck Furniture, later known as Kinleigh & August's Attic and Ladybug Treasures
Married to Kinleigh Scott, father of Vivian, brother of Caleb and Ivy

Beckett Manning: Owns Happy Acres Orchard
Brother to Zoe, Hayes, and Justin

Ben Sullivan: EMT/Drummer

Bess Wainwright:
Grandmother of Asher Wainwright, great-grandmother of Lily and Rose

Bonnie Ramos: Sheriff's department dispatcher
Married to Enrique Ramos, mother of Damien, Erica, Francesca, Gabriela, and Regina, grandmother of Samantha and Leo

Bryce Johnson: Professor
Best friends with Callum MacGregor

Caleb Beck: Teaches second grade at the Catholic school
Brother of August and Ivy

(Charles) Dare Kramer: Mechanic, owns J & T Body Shop, later known as Kramer & Burns Custom
Married to Kelsey Ford, father of Weston and Sean, brother of Gage

Callum MacGregor: Adjunct mythology professor/painter
Married to Ellie Lawton, father of Faith Mistletoe, brother of Lennox, Hudson, and Finn, best friends with Bryce Johnson

Christian Masterson: Sheriff's deputy
Brother of Murphy, Travis, Penn, and Madison

Cindy Ford:

Married to Doug Ford, mother of Kelsey and Rylee, grandmother of Weston, Sean, and Hayley

Colette Edison: Owns Every Line A Story, art supply and yarn shop

Dahlia McKenna: Designer/decorator who works with Macy

Damien Ramos: Carpenter
Brother of Erica, Francesca, Gabriela, and Regina

Doug Ford:
Married to Cindy Ford, father of Kelsey and Rylee, grandfather of Weston, Sean, and Hayley

Ellie Lawton: Hair stylist/works at Brewed Awakening
Married to Callum MacGregor, mother of Faith Mistletoe

Enrique Ramos:
Married to Bonnie Ramos, father of Damien, Erica, Francesca, Gabriela, and Regina, grandfather of Samantha and Leo

Erica Ramos: Owns Sharkey's
Married to Jacob Mills, mother of Leo, sister of Damien, Francesca, Gabriela, and Regina,

Finn MacGregor: Architect
Brother of Lennox, Hudson, and Finn

Francesca Ramos: Involved in the fashion industry in NYC
Sister of Damien, Erica, Gabriela, and Regina

Gavin Forrester: Real estate owner

Gabriela Ramos: Co-owner Hannah's Helping Hands

Sister of Damien, Erica, Francesca, and Regina, best friends with Hannah Jacobs

George Beck:
Married to Annie Beck, father of August, Caleb, and Ivy, grandfather of Rhiannon and Vivian

Greta Conrad: Manager of the Rusty Spoon

Hank Masterson:
Married to JoAnn Masterson, father of Murphy, Christian, Travis, Penn, and Madison, grandfather of Carrington, Brayden, and twins Theodore and Elijah

Hannah Jacobs: Owns Hannah's Helping Hands
Married to Asher Wainwright, mother of Lily and Rose, best friends with Gabriela Ramos

Hayes Manning: Owns Happy Acres orchard
Brother of Zoe, Beckett, and Justin

Hudson MacGregor: Graphic designer
Brother of Callum, Lennox, and Finn

Ian Kagan: Solo artist
Engaged to Zoe Manning, father of Elvis, brother of Simon, best friends with Rory Ferguson, friends with Flynn Sheppard and Kellan McGuire

Ivy Beck: Waitress at the Rusty Spoon and owns Rolling Cones ice cream truck
Married to Rory Ferguson, mother of Rhiannon, sister of August and Caleb, best friends with Kinleigh Scott, friends with Maggie Kelly and Zoe Manning

Jacob Mills: Firefighter/Fire Code Chief
Married to Erica Ramos, father of Leo, brother of Kayla

James Hamilton: Owns Hamilton Realty
Father of twins Seth and Oliver, grandfather of Laurie, Alexander, and Star

Jared Brooks: Sheriff
Engaged to Gina Ramos, father of Samantha, brother of Mason

Jessica Gideon: Actress
Ex-wife to John Gideon, mother to Dani

JoAnn Masterson:
Married to Hank Masterson, mother of Murphy, Christian, Travis, Penn, and Madison, grandmother of Carrington, Brayden, and twins Theodore and Elijah

John Gideon: Owns Gideon Gets it Done handyman service
Married to Macy Devereaux, father of Dani and Michael, ex-wife Jessica Gideon

Justin Manning: Owns Happy Acres Orchard
Brother of Zoe, Beckett, and Hayes

Kellan McGuire: Lead singer Wilder Mind, solo artist
Married to Maggie Kelly, father of Wolf, brother of Bethany, friends with Rory Ferguson, Ian Kagan, and Myles Vaughn

Kelsey Ford: Elementary school teacher
Married to Dare Kramer, mother of Sean, stepson Weston, sister of Rylee

Kinleigh Scott: Owns Kinleigh's Attic, later known as Kinleigh & August's Attic
Married to August Beck, mother to Vivian, cousin of Vincent Scott, best friends with Ivy Beck

Kylie Fisher: Bartender
Involved with Justin Norton, lives in Forrester Apartments

Lennox MacGregor: Lawyer
Brother of Callum, Finn, and Hudson

(Lucas) Gage Kramer: Former race car driver, owns Kramer & Burns Custom
Married to Rylee Ford, father of Hayley, brother of Dare

Lucky Roberts: Works for Gideon Gets it Done Handyman Service

Luna Hastings: Works at Kinleigh's Attic,
later known as Kinleigh & August's Attic, tarot card reader
Friends with Kinleigh Scott, Gina Ramos, April Finley, and Ryan Moon

Macy Devereaux: Owns Brewed Awakening and The Haunt
Married to John Gideon, stepmother of Dani, mother of Michael, sister of Nolan, best friends with Rylee Ford

Madison 'Maddie' Masterson:
Sister of Murphy, Christian, Travis, and Penn

Marjorie Hamilton:
Ex-wife of Seth Hamilton, birth mother of Laurie

Mason Brooks: Owns Mason Jar restaurant
Brother to Jared Brooks

Maggie Kelly:
Married to Kellan McGuire, mother of Wolf, best friends with Kendra Russo, friends with Ivy Beck and Zoe Manning

Melissa Kramer: Owns Robbie's Pizza
Married to Robert Kramer, mother of Dare and Gage, grandmother of Weston, Sean, and Hayley

Mike London: High school teacher

Mitch Cooper: Owns the Rusty Spoon

Murphy 'Moose' Masterson: Game designer/construction contractor and owns Baby Daddy Wanted
Married to Vee Dixon, father of Brayden and twins Theodore and Elijah, brother of Christian, Travis, Penn, and Madison

Nolan Devereaux: Owns Tricks and Treats candy shop
Brother of Macy

Oliver Hamilton: Owns Hamilton Realty and the Hummingbird's Nest
Married to Sage Evans, father of Star, twin brother of Seth

Paisley Jones: Works at To Dye For hair salon

Penn Masterson: Graphic novelist
Brother of Murphy, Travis, Christian, and Madison

Regina 'Gina' Ramos: Waitress at the Rusty Spoon
Engaged to Jared Brooks, mother of Samantha, sister of Damien, Erica, Francesca, and Gabriela

Robert Kramer: Owns Robbie's Pizza
Married to Melissa Kramer, father of Dare and Gage, grandfather of Weston, Sean and Hayley

Rory Ferguson: Record producer/rhythm guitarist
Married to Ivy Beck, father of Rhiannon, brother of Thomas and Maureen, best friends with Ian Kagan, friends with Flynn Sheppard and Kellan McGuire

Ryan Moon: Artist and tarot card reader
Friends with Kinleigh Scott, Luna Hastings, and April Finley

Rylee Ford: Barista at Brewed Awakening

Married to Gage Kramer, mother of Hayley, sister of Kelsey, best friends with Macy Devereaux

Sage Evans: Owns the Hummingbird's Nest
Married to Oliver Hamilton, mother of Star, best friends with Ally Lawrence

Seth Hamilton: Owns Hamilton Realty
Married to Ally Lawrence, father of Laurie and Alexander, twin brother of Oliver, ex-wife Marjorie

Tabitha Monaghan: Owns Sugar Rush bakery

Tish Burns: Owns Kramer & Burns Custom, custom fabricator
Friends with Gage Kramer

Travis Masterson:
Father of Carrington, brother of Christian, Penn, Murphy, and Madison

Veronica 'Vee' Dixon: Pastry baker at Brewed Awakening, owns Baby Daddy Wanted
Married to Murphy Masterson, mother of Brayden and twins Theodore and Elijah, friends with Macy Devereaux

Vincent Scott: partner in Wainwright Publishing Industries
Cousin of Kinleigh Scott

Zoe Manning: Artist/photographer
Engaged to Ian Kagan, mother of Elvis, sister of Beckett, Hayes, and Justin, cousin of Lila Ronson Shawcross Crandall, friends with Ivy Beck and Maggie Kelly

as of 02/12/2021

CRESCENT COVE

Have My Baby

Claim My Baby

Who's The Daddy

Pit Stop: Baby

Baby Daddy Wanted

Rockstar Baby

Daddy in Disguise

My Ex's Baby

Daddy Undercover

Wrong Bed Baby

CRESCENT COVE STANDALONES

CEO Daddy

CRESCENT COVE BITES

Fireman Daddy

Mistletoe Baby

For more information about our books visit

www.tarynquinn.com

ALSO BY TARYN QUINN

AFTERNOON DELIGHT

Dirty Distractions

Drawn Deep

DEUCES WILD

Protecting His Rockstar

Guarding His Best Friend's Sister

Shielding His Baby

WILDER ROCK

Rockstar Daddy

Rockstar Lost

HOLIDAY BOOKS

Unwrapped

Holiday Sparks

Filthy Scrooge

Bad Kitty

Saving Kylie

For more information about our books visit

www.tarynquinn.com

ABOUT TARYN QUINN

USA Today bestselling author, TARYN QUINN, is the redheaded stepchild of bestselling authors Taryn Elliott & Cari Quinn. We've been writing together for a lifetime—wait, no it's really been only a handful of years, but we have a lot of fun. Sometimes we write stories that don't quite fit into our regular catalog.

* Ultra sexy—check.
* Quirky characters—check.
* Sweet–usually mixed in with the sexy...so, yeah—check.
* RomCom—check.
* Dark and twisted—check.

A little something for everyone.

So, c'mon in. Light some candles, pour a glass of wine...maybe even put on some sexy music.

For more information about us...
tarynquinn.com
tq@tarynquinn.com

QUINN AND ELLIOTT

We also write more serious, longer, and sexier books as Cari Quinn & Taryn Elliott. Our topics include mostly rockstars, but mobsters, MMA, and a little suspense gets tossed in there too.

Rockers' Series Reading Order

Lost in Oblivion

Winchester Falls

Found in Oblivion

Hammered

Rock Revenge

Brooklyn Dawn

OTHER SERIES

The Boss

Tapped Out

Love Required

Boys of Fall

If you'd like more information about us please visit

www.quinnandelliott.com

www.ingramcontent.com/pod-product-compliance
Lightning Source LLC
Chambersburg PA
CBHW061243170626
46809CB00007B/2801